ASCENSION

Portrait of a Woman

Dana Walker Lindley

CONTENTS

Title Page

Dedication

Author's Note

Escape   1

Opportunity   6

Challenge   15

Mission   30

Kinship   43

Meltdown   49

Story   55

Preparations   66

Derby   75

Survival   82

Graduation   96

Clarity   101

Flyboy   116

Duty   122

Reunion   133

Revelation   147

News   165

Recovery   173

Story   181

Diversion   207

Resilience   219

Dismissal   234

Horizon   244

About The Author   255

ACKNOWLEDGEMENTS   257

AUTHOR'S NOTE

To tell this story, I used fictional and historical characters that explore universal truths. Although inspired by actual events, this novel evolved solely from my imagination informed by research. This book is fiction. Thank you for reading Ascension. If you would like to correspond, email me at Ascensiondwl@gmail.com.

ESCAPE

Chapter One

Never before have we had so little time in which to do so much.

PRESIDENT FRANKLIN D. ROOSEVELT

❉ ❉ ❉

M arch 1943

"Name?"

"Colleen O'Brie...Donnelly."

The sergeant's bald head looked up from the form on his desk for the first time since she entered the room. He stared with tired eyes. "It's usually not a difficult question, Miss O'Brie? Donnelly?"

"Colleen Donnelly."

"Birth date?"

"January 14, 1921."

He scrawled numbers into tiny boxes.

"Married?"

"Well, uh…"

"Once more, Miss Donnelly, it's a simple question. Married, yes, or no?"

"Well, yes and no," she stammered, face flushed red. She resented having to reveal her secrets to the first man she meets. Too raw, too shameful. Not in the mood to explain.

Sergeant Bentley put down his pen and stared. "Which is it, Colleen Donnelly, are you or are you not married?" The firmness in his voice meant no nonsense.

She'd known Tommy O'Brien since they'd played together in the courtyard sandbox, while their mothers sat on her shaded stoop or his, drinking iced tea, sharing gossip and solving all the problems in the neighborhood. The brownstones that sheltered them, their parents, three Irish grandmothers and two grandfathers, stood next door to each other on the corner of Spring Street and Acadia Avenue. She'd lived beside him every day of her life.

Of course, she'd married him.

But was she still? Married?

"Married, legally, but I filed for divorce last week."

"Explain."

"I am legally married, but I left my husband last week."

"You just said that. You should know we do not

accept married women, Mrs. Donnelly. Go home and resume life with your husband."

The right side of her face still ached from that last blow. Her jaw made a new grinding noise when she talked, so she hadn't said much since last Sunday, when all hell broke loose. This was all too hard, too sudden.

"Colleen Donnelly O'Brien. Mrs. O'Brien. I will never go back to him."

The sergeant's eyes looked directly into hers, not flinching. He cleared his throat, cleaned his glasses and replaced them on his nose. He'd heard it all before and continued questioning in the same routine manner.

"Children?"

"A daughter, Chloe, she's three and a half."

"Mrs. O'Brien, why are you wasting my time? You must know we don't enlist married women or mothers of young children. You're at Bowman Field Air Base applying to the School of Air Evacuation in the U.S Army Air Force. You're applying to be a flight nurse for the military, not a nanny."

She placed her hospital name badge before him on the form. "Sir, I am a registered nurse, fully trained at Cornell University School of Nursing. I have the skills you need. You have the job I need."

"Reporting from where, Nurse O'Brien?" Her assertiveness impressed him; some new recruits were intimidated by the army's hierarchy of command.

"Cornell Medical Center. Just finished the last two years of my clinicals delivering babies. I don't suppose you do much of that here." Her smile reflected the poignancy of placing freshly born daughters and sons on their mothers' bare breasts in the most tender minutes. She could smell the wetness of their slippery bodies, hear the gurgle of their suckling, mother and child connecting instinctively, naturally, on the most profound and fundamental level.

She pressed forward, pretending confidence while her insides roiled and lips trembled, her body in full fight or flight mode. Fear was the cudgel; fear of Tommy's fist, fear of losing Chloe, fear of hunger and poverty. Fear had compelled her to this dreadful moment.

Sergeant Bentley closed the file. "You have a child and husband back in Ithaca, Nurse O'Brien. You should go home, take care of them."

"I can't, sir, not now, not yet. I have to get away. I have to earn my living. I want to take care of my daughter. I want to take care of patients and stand on my own two feet. That's what I should do. That's why I am here, to support the war effort. The U. S. Army hires nurses, doesn't it? Hire me."

She had never spoken with such bluntness; it's shocking how much fury a fist in the eye arouses.

The phone rang, interrupting them, then once more. A harried corporal leaned in the door briefly to comment on the applicant before Colleen. Finally, a weary Sergeant Bentley sighed before signing the dotted line and handing the form and file to her.

"Nurse O'Brien, I am an admitting clerk with no authority to change the rules, which clearly state you are not eligible. But we've been slammed the last twelve months since the war heated up. We're short nurses. Without them, men die. Report to Captain Dorsey, Terminal One. If you can convince him, he will find a place for you. God knows, when the lives of our boys are on the line, I'm willing to bend a few rules."

OPPORTUNITY

Chapter Two

*We must be the great arsenal
of democracy.*

PRESIDENT FRANKLIN D. ROOSEVELT

❖ ❖ ❖

I sure don't care about rules, Colleen thought as she crossed the quadrangle toward Captain Dorsey's headquarters. Maybe she didn't care about much of anything now, except Chloe. She had always done what she was supposed to do. She took Chloe to Sunday Mass, devoted every spare moment to her family, earned wages at Cornell, even planted a garden. She obeyed, met expectations, said "yes". She did her best, not perfectly, but her best.

She had followed the rules. It was Tommy who broke them, who made a mess of their lives. *I'm not supposed to be apart from Chloe. I'm a wife, a mother. I am supposed to be home, in Ithaca with my family, not in Kentucky with strangers.*

Tommy O'Brien had smashed her face first on New Year's Day when he was still hungover from drinking at Flanagan's Bar the night before. They argued about the steam inhaler she had bought for Chloe, after Dr. Tafel recommended it. With that and Vick's VapoRub, the baby's congested lungs had cleared. Colleen's sin was not asking Tommy's permission first. She took the slam as a warning, in shock, in secret, in a deep state of hurt and denial.

Fifty-nine days later, that same fist knocked her to the floor, the back of her head cracking on the table's edge on the way down. When she came to, Tommy stood over her, hands clenched, fierce rage flashing in his face. Chloe sat crying on her, wretched with fright.

That image of her husband and child led her directly to her parent's door to bear the surprised but knowing look on Mama's face. Colleen stood there holding her books, stethoscope and a sobbing Chloe, whose tiny hand squeezed hers. Mama required no explanation. Mary Caroline Donnelly hugged them both and ushered them in. Colleen was her youngest, and though Mama and Papa had danced at her wedding, and the weddings of the first five, too, they would always welcome her home.

Mama put a pan on the stove and lit the fire. She filled it with soup from the evening meal, reheated a roll and set it on the table beside the fruit. Colleen could not eat, but she held Chloe and soothed her, blowing on the hot liquid to cool it before spooning small drops into her child's open mouth. As the baby ate, she wrapped her arms tightly around Colleen to keep her close, unwilling to let go. When her tummy was full, Granny Donnelly rocked her dear grandchild until she slept in her arms, then tucked her in tightly on the bed with the pastel blue pillows.

"Mama, I can't stay here," Colleen said when she returned to the kitchen table carrying two hot cups of tea. "I must leave for a while. I can't be in the same room with Tommy O'Brien, not even the same town. I can't face him, or his sister when I go to Stockton's, or all the wives. The men at the factory were already talking about us after the incident there."

"What are you going to do?"

"I'm joining the army."

"What on earth are you saying? You are not joining the army, Colleen. The army is at war. You are not going to war."

"The army is hiring nurses, Mama. I'm proficient in obstetrics but need to expand my skills and become more competent in other areas. If they hire me, I'll earn a higher salary and get benefits, too. With what I learn there, I'll be able to find a good job when I come home."

"They'll ship you off somewhere, Colleen, somewhere far from here, somewhere dangerous. What will you do then? And what will you do with Chloe? Who will take care of her?"

"Look at me, Mama. I can't take care of myself. I'm no good for Chloe right now and I can't take her with me. Please, Mama, look after her for me for a little while, until I can care for Chloe myself."

Mama started to protest but knew Colleen was right. Chloe would be safe and well-loved, and Colleen must find a means to leave Tommy O'Brien, once and for all. Resigned, Mama fixed a sack lunch for the long Greyhound bus ride and helped her daughter pack three bags for her stay in Louisville.

The following morning after a fitful night, Mama's bountiful breakfast and Chloe's searing good-by, Papa drove Colleen to the station. He had fought in World War I and knew better than she did the horror of what she would face. He heaved in fear and sadness at the idea of his beloved girl entering that world.

But she sensed his pride, too, that she would commit her talent to minister to the injured fellows who would come into her custody. What would he have given for a nurse like her when the bullet pierced his right thigh and left him with a step-splat-step limp for the rest of his life? She would, Papa knew, use her compassion and competence to give every man the help his spirit warranted, and his body needed, to let healing begin. Knowing this and pondering all, he held her near, kissed her head and whispered through choked tears, "I love you, Collie, you come back to me, ok? No matter what, remember that you are my baby girl, and I will always love you."

With her last look, she saw the tears rolling down his face, reflected in the sun. *If I live to be a thousand, I'll never have a husband who loves me as much as Papa loves Mama. They are devoted to each other. I'm lucky they are devoted to me, too.*

Colleen tried to squelch the memory so she could practice for her interview with Captain Dorsey. She would enunciate clearly as Nurse Plimpton had insisted. "Clarity means everything to your patient's well-being," Nurse Plimpton would repeat. "When you advocate for your patients, make sure the doctor knows what you want to say. Speak up, Nurse." She would speak up to the captain, too.

Following an abrupt, "Report!" shouted from Captain Dorsey's office, Colleen walked into a modest, drab green room lined with metal file cabinets. A picture of President Roosevelt hung over the door. The captain sat behind a standard-issue desk, the bottom left drawer hanging open, jammed and broken. But his military discipline and professional decorum dominated this room. Everything was in order.

Here, through the decisions he made, he changed the course of women's lives and saved injured soldiers in battles not yet fought. Hour after hour, in an unrelenting effort, he worked to provide the Army Air Force what they demanded of him; 60,000 highly qualified nurses.

He took the folder from her and reviewed it. "Nurse O'Brien, I see Sergeant Bentley recommends you for service. Tell me, what are your qualifications?"

"I attended Cornell University School of Nursing and completed my clinicals, working in obstetrics at the medical center. But I did rotations in every unit–surgery, pediatrics, intensive care–everything but psychiatry. I know how to clean and bandage wounds, read vitals, administer meds, draw blood and provide emergency care."

"Ever been on an airplane?"

"No, sir."

"Done calisthenics?"

"Baby playtime exercises for the last two years, no calisthenics."

He looked at her, evaluated her, checked for a smirk. Detecting none, he continued.

"Ever seen bodies shattered by guns? Bones crushed? Limbs blown off, every vessel sheared open and bleeding?"

"No sir, but I spent four months helping fragile, premature quadruplets breathe. I know how to nurture life, how to give my assistance, how to care."

"This is the headquarters for an air base and bomber squadron. Do you realize what we do here? That we train military nurses to command air evacuation operations? Our personnel will be assigned to the front in the South Pacific immediately upon graduation. Are you prepared to go to the front, Mrs. O'Brien? To risk your life? To not see your daughter?"

Of course not, she thought, *I'm not brave. Three days ago, I was content to be in Ithaca handing new-*

borns to their exhausted and ecstatic mothers. I'm a mom, a wife, a nurse. I came to Kentucky because I won't take another blow. I came because I need a job and a home, so I can shape a new life for Chloe and me.

"Sir, I am a good nurse. What I don't know, I will learn. I am here because you asked nurses to serve the war effort. I am here because I love my daughter. Surely, I can be both a patriotic American and a good mother at the same time?"

He studied her. "You're right, Nurse O'Brien, you can be both. I see from the letters written by your references that you are well regarded by your superiors. However, while your credentials are exceptional, the U.S. Army does not induct women into the School of Air Evacuation who are married with young children. Nevertheless, I must hire nurses. Would you be willing to serve faithfully and well in a civilian position at the base hospital?"

"You mean stay in Louisville?"

"On the base, at Nichols General, the other side of Bowman Field. You can start today at 1500 hours, second shift, and perform a variety of auxiliary roles, whatever Captain Chantel has for you. There's plenty to do. It may not be the adventure you thought you were signing up for, your feet will never leave the ground, but you will play a vital role and serve the war effort."

"How do I find her?"

"She's the one with the most stripes on her cap, third floor."

"Of course, yes sir. Thank you, sir. It's perfect sir. You won't regret it."

"I'm sure I won't. Report to Captain Chantel. She'll assign you," he said, handing her the folder of documents, the top one bearing his signature. "The war demands our finest, doesn't it, Nurse? You won't disappoint our soldiers. You won't disappoint yourself. And you won't disappoint General MacArthur."

"No, sir, I'm pleased to have this chance. I won't disappoint you or the General." She smiled, nodded and exited quickly into a hallway lined with nervous women wearing anxious smiles, holding folders as full of expectation as hers.

He thinks I seek adventure, she thought, heading across campus. *He has no idea how relieved I am that I don't have to fly overseas. Do I look like a soldier? I'm not like these strong, fit, courageous women I see marching in formation, their crisp blue uniforms perfectly creased. I seek security for Chloe, a meal on the table and a fire in the fireplace, not a medal.*

Colleen arrived at Nichols General Hospital, third floor, at precisely 1400 hours and waited patiently at the desk until the clerk acknowledged her. "I'm Colleen O'Brien. I'd like to meet with Captain Chantel." She placed the form bearing Captain Dorsey's signature on the desk.

"Why, wouldn't we all, sugar," the woman replied in a southern twang as thick as honey, barely glancing at the paper but shining a wide smile in Colleen's direction. "Now if you have all day, go sit in her office and find yourself a Better Homes and Gardens magazine to update your decorating style. If you don't, and you're a nurse, check in at that station down the hall and make yourself useful."

"I haven't been assigned yet."

"Doesn't matter, you will be. Captain Chantel will be fixin' you up real soon. We don't have a minute to waste, and you're more likely to catch her in a patient's room than in her office."

"But I don't have my uniform with me."

"Don't worry, it's provided. Find the storage room on the first floor in the back. There's plenty to choose from on the rack. The cafeteria is serving biscuits and gravy today. Best to grab a bite before you start your shift. Probably won't get a chance to fill your breadbasket the rest of the night." Then the sweet-looking young woman with a long, blonde braid returned to her task, pencil in hand.

Uniforms provided! That's a good deal, Colleen considered as she walked down the back stairs into the storage room. She pulled out the first size ten she found. When she tried it on, the white starched uniform fit like it was made for her, with plenty of pockets for her stethoscope and whatever else she found necessary to carry. She admired her reflection in the mirror for a moment. No one looks sharper than a nurse in full dress. Unless it's an entire airfield of well-conditioned women wearing the functional, dignified clothing of a Second Lieutenant Air Evacuation Nurse.

CHALLENGE

Chapter Three

*If a problem cannot be
solved, enlarge it.*

GENERAL DWIGHT D. EISENHOWER

❖ ❖ ❖

Colleen finished a quick meal sitting at the end of a long table filled with doctors, nurses, med techs and clerical staff. Their animated faces engaged in lively conversation with each other during this break in their shifts. They spoke about a young airman who was learning to walk again after the amputation of his left leg; of the doctors and nurses who endured a grueling, eighteen-hour surgery on a grunt after he sustained multiple injuries in a motorcycle accident; and of the release of a favored patient, the happy-go-lucky young man who always managed a smile and a joke for everyone, despite his pain.

She left the cafeteria and walked down the

hallway past the rooms, appraising the actions of the staff, the patient count and the locations of supplies. When she landed at the main station, she stated her name as the phone rang. The nurse, whose badge read H. Anderson, RN, checked a box on a list, smiled a "Welcome" while answering the phone, then said, "Check on 302" without missing a beat.

Colleen entered room 302 and saw to her dismay the battered body of a twenty-seven-year-old pilot, Gregory Hutch, patched from one end to the other by the capable surgeons at Nichols General. An engine had stalled in a B-18 Bolo during a routine practice flight. He'd crashed, nose first. He had avoided the power lines along Taylorsville Road but couldn't avoid the hard earth that rose to meet him. He fell among propellers, wheels and parts that still littered the ground. He was fortunate to survive, though immobile and unaware.

His injuries were so severe, she felt momentarily stunned. She didn't know where to begin; he was battered beyond what anyone could expect to survive. But despite his broken bones and excruciating pain, the spark of life she saw in him convinced her he had a chance. She started by straightening the sheets and repositioning his body, taking his vitals, checking his meds, adjusting his equipment, wetting his lips, bathing his face and massaging with lotion whatever bare skin she could find.

"Hi, Greg," she whispered, when she saw his eyelids flutter. "You're in the hospital, Nichols General, at Bowman Field. You're a little banged up, but you're in good hands now. Just relax, Buddy, let me take care of you. With your help, we'll get you feeling better in no time."

She wasn't sure he could hear her, but she continued to speak to him in the calm and comforting tone she knew soothed the frightened. She had discovered that her gift as a nurse was an instinctive recognition of what each patient needed, and how she could provide that comfort. She had used it to keep alive four tiny, identical bodies covered with barely-there flesh, struggling to breathe through lungs as delicate as a butterfly's wings. This brought the most satisfaction in her profession, knowing someone breathed easier because of her.

There were other moments that day when her knees shook at the shocking sights of badly broken men, but each time she calmed herself, steadied her nerves and regained control. After spending the afternoon tending to other patients on the floor, she briefly met with Captain Chantel, whose hat bore the two black stripes of Chief Nurse. The captain transferred Colleen to the emergency room, which always needed more nurses than the hospital could spare. There she stitched cuts, dressed burns, assisted with a dislocated shoulder. She'd seen it all before at Cornell and was pleasantly surprised how solid her skills remained.

It was nearly 2200 before she saw Captain Chantel again. Colleen was addressing the injuries of three young brothers, the sheriff's sons, who were temporarily indisposed due to some foolish behavior. Sheriff Hamilton preferred to bring his boys to Nichols when necessary and left them with her while he fetched his wife.

"Ah, Nurse O'Brien, how are you doing?" Chantel asked, entering the room. She observed Colleen's quick hands as they removed the objects the boys had shoved up their noses. "I see you've gotten acquainted and found your way around." The trumpet in her voice cut through the chatter.

"Yes, Captain, the staff has been wonderful helping me find everything I need."

"Good. You still have much to know about how we do things, but that will come in the next few weeks on the job. Ask questions, learn as you go."

Colleen retrieved the last bean from the last boy's nose and used the large hand mirror to show the three of them the bruised and swollen faces their prank had caused.

"Now spread your legs and stand tall, go on, all of you," she ordered. The boys reluctantly shuffled to the corners of the small room to stand on straight legs, looking at her with quizzical expressions.

"Put your arms up above your head. Good. Straighten your hands, act like you're reaching for the sun. Stretch hard, really stretch. Breathe deeply in, out. See how good it feels when air flows through your lungs? Remember that from now on, keep your noses clean," she said, ushering them from the room into the arms of their parents, who were pleased that no serious harm was done and determined to hold them accountable.

Colleen returned to Captain Chantel. "Where will I be assigned, Captain?"

"I will assess you before I decide that. For now, check with Anderson each day. She'll partner with you while you get your bearings. Do as she says. I'll let you know soon about a permanent placement."

"Thank you. I'll report to her tomorrow at 0800."

"See that you do. And O'Brien, you don't have family here, right?"

"No, Ma'am, no I don't," she stuttered.

"You're not obligated to live on base. You can rent a nicely furnished room with a shared bath near the hospital for around $3.00 a week, $3.50 if you eat breakfast. But we have some accommodations for the nurses here. Check them out, if you're interested. Nothing fancy, but they're free, and it makes getting here promptly a breeze. Better still, it's close enough that you'll be able to collapse in bed ten minutes after your shift ends. Sleep is scarce here, so that becomes rather significant."

"I'd like that very much. I'm trying to save money."

"You'll receive $840 per year, same as the Second Lieutenants, but you'll have little chance to

19

spend it. Eat your meals in the mess. See Deloris, first floor, to check out equipment. Consider yourself on call 24/7."

"I will," Colleen said, "and I'll work hard for you. All the activity today was a bit overwhelming, but I'll get used to it."

"There are days that overwhelm us all," Captain Chantel said. "Expect it. Ask for help when necessary. I trust you know, O'Brien, what an honor it is to serve in this hospital. Some of our patients are the brave men who are a part of this great war. Many are young, many have been to hell and back. It's our job to meet them where they are and help them rebound and renew. They'll live some of the sorriest moments of their lives here with us, without the benefit of their families to console them. We make sure to give them what they need."

"I've seen examples of that already. I'm alone here, too. I can be family for them as well."

"We'll see. It's not always easy. You will drill at 0700 tomorrow. We emphasize the importance of physical and mental fitness with our staff. You will see that our jobs are emotionally, as well as physically, demanding, probably more than what you're used to. Take care of yourself and stay in shape. The doctor will examine you afterwards to update your vaccines for typhoid and tetanus," Captain Chantel said as she exited through the door.

The shift passed quickly, and when it was

over, Colleen dropped her suitcases on the floor by the empty bed in the corner of the barracks. For privacy, the other residents had designed temporary, individual barriers; clever screens built from cardboard boxes, stacks of luggage, drapes of clothing, whatever they could find around their cots to create a separate space, and in some cases, a bit of luxury. Her area was no larger than a prison cell, but these walls wouldn't contain her. She claimed a bed for resting and a place to dress. This would do.

She fell on her bunk in a mixture of exhaustion from the day's labor and the fiery fatigue stoked by the wrenching decisions of the past few days. Colleen still felt keenly Tommy's jarring jab to her eye, and the knockout slam she'd inflicted on herself when she handed Chloe to Mama and turned to walk away. She started to shiver.

Freezing her was the realization that the life shared with her husband and daughter in the small bungalow was no more. Gone, too, were her colleagues at Cornell, her best friends, really, people she'd entrust her life to. They had earned their closeness through stories told during long hours of laboring love, and those awesome moments when a new mom was rescued from near-death by quick action, clear thinking and the cooperation of the entire team. She may not see those women again.

They had tended their patients side by side for two years and knew each other's movements by rote. They also knew Colleen was the one who often accepted the opportunities Cornell offered for advanced education, that she would be a competent replacement for Nurse Hackett, who would retire in the next year or two. They questioned why Colleen would resign suddenly and leave them, but they didn't question her resolve, carried deep within her strong shoulders and the same long, limber legs that held her steady as she embraced punchy mothers until new life bloomed.

They didn't know for sure, but suspected her quick departure had something to do with that hothead, Tommy O'Brien. Marion had been present once when Tommy looked as if he wouldn't hold back if Colleen somehow stood in his way. It was always curious to her that a woman as smart as Colleen didn't see it, too.

Colleen pulled the green blanket up to her chin and rolled her head on the pillow. Most lights were out, but a few dim bulbs burned throughout the huge room. Soft music from NBC radio hummed in the ears of someone stretched out under her identical green blanket. Colleen didn't have a radio but wouldn't listen if she did. She didn't have the endurance. She didn't want to hear the bad news the announcer read between songs. She didn't want to know what city had been destroyed, didn't want to hear a body count. She wanted to fall into a deep slumber but couldn't. Her mind raced.

I'm earning more wages than I did as a baby

nurse, and more than the Public Health Department pays, or the state sanitorium, or the Visiting Nurses, she calculated. *I don't have to buy my uniforms, so that's another $5.00 a month I won't have to spend. With free room and board, nearly every penny I make can go in my bank account. Every dollar saved buys my ticket back to Chloe and our new home.*

She repeated these facts until her mind grew numb to the day's anxieties, slightly soothed by solid numbers. She trusted them; they supported her goals.

When the 0500-alarm blared, Colleen bolted upright and tried to reorient herself to this place; the small bed with the flimsy mattress, well used, the cold air blowing in around the tall windows, the high metal ceilings reflecting noises she didn't recognize. *Holy cow, I slept in my clothes and didn't unpack. I've got to shower, dress and eat before reporting to drill. I'm already late and don't want to blow it on my first full day.* With that she quickly moved from making her bed to sorting her case for a bra and underwear to carry to the showers in the middle of the hall.

Each of the ten stalls was occupied, so she brushed her hair and teeth while waiting. There was no point visiting with the others, they were as hurried as she, but each extended courtesies her way. "The hook on that door is broken. You'll have to hold the bottom with your foot if you want to keep it closed," said the woman she'd seen two bunks over, the one with the collection of small tables covered with framed photos of the large extended family she left behind in North Carolina.

Another advised not to use the soap from the dispensary. "Honestly, the first week I was here, I washed my face with it and broke out in a terrible rash. I was embarrassed to be seen in public, thought I'd startle the patients or get fired for suspicion of leprosy," she warned, smiling like a woman sitting on a beach with a book, radiating sunny contentment.

"I left in a hurry, without doing a lot of shopping," Colleen replied. "I didn't bring my personal soap with me."

"Here, take a share of mine, until you can buy some," the woman said, handing her a small chunk. "I'll take you shopping on Frankfort Avenue your first day off. You can pay me back then. I'm Elizabeth from the Show Me state. Call me Liz."

"Thanks, Liz, I'd like that. The last thing I want is a face full of zits. I'm Colleen. Ithaca, New York."

"Well, you better hurry up, Colleen. I'm finished, take my stall. I don't know who the drill sarge is today, but all of them make you, and often the rest of us, pay if you hold up the group. Meet up in the mess if you can, I'll save a place for you."

"I'll be there. What do you recommend for breakfast?"

Elizabeth laughed. "Oh, hon, that's sweet. There is no recommending. You take what you get. It's hot and plain but edible. Just don't think you're going to be selecting from a menu."

Determined to not be late, Colleen raced through her morning ritual and arrived at the dining hall with ten minutes to spare. She stood in a quick line, then walked to Elizabeth's table, placed her tray on it and swung her legs under to fit.

"Glad you made it," Liz said. "Eat plenty before your shift, so you can make it through the day."

"I learned that yesterday," Colleen said, savoring her first swig of coffee, black, no sugar, "don't think I stopped once until it was over. It's not like that every day, is it?"

"We have the occasional lull, but yes, mostly we're always running. Chantel won't tolerate a lazy nurse, and the guys who come through here are just great, the greatest. We want to give them all we've got in return. We're so thankful for all they do."

"I'm used to birthing babies, lots of waiting before lots of action. I think I'm going to like this, though, it's always exciting. Does it ever get to be too much?"

"Almost every day. But you sleep and wake up to the next one. A good thing about our work is that it's never done. Someone always needs us. Why did you leave the babies to come here?"

"To serve my country, then to return by the quickest possible route and snuggle my little girl. Birthing babies won't pay the bills, nursing here will. And when I return to Ithaca, surgeons who depend on their nurses pay three times what birthing mommas can afford, which is often nothing."

"I know what you mean. Sounds like you've got a solid plan that will get you where you want to be."

"Yea, I think so. I would have asked Captain Dorsey to assign me to a battlefield if that's what it takes to earn a position like this. Heck, I'd jump out of an airplane, if necessary. I need to be able to support both of us."

"It's a good thing you won't need a parachute. This is the best opportunity you could ask for to improve your competency and serve your country, too."

Both women stacked their trays and headed to the hill in a gentle jog. In March, the outlines of Kentucky's natural beauty were evident everywhere. The sun shone like a crystal chandelier dangling in the middle of a Monet blue sky. Clouds floated overhead. A cool breeze cleansed the air. Colleen inhaled deeply and said a prayer of appreciation for the stamina necessary to complete her duties and the support of colleagues to get through her day. After all she'd lost, she still had that, an opportunity.

She should have prayed for help getting through drill practice. Jumping Jacks. Push-ups. "Hup 2, 3, 4," bellowed Drill Sergeant Chouse as they marched. "Head up, spine straight, suck your belly in, swing those arms, lift your knees, step high, step high." For the next hour she did exactly that, covering four miles with as much enthusiasm as she could muster.

"My legs are wobbly and my feet hurt," Colleen complained to Elizabeth as they left the field on the way back to the barracks. "I've not exercised that hard since, since, well, not ever. The last time I ran was the second leg of the relay race at the county fair. That was high school."

"Wait until you have to carry your pack." Elizabeth laughed. "It might just flatten you. We'll have to scrape you up and mold you into the shape of a woman."

"Do we do this every morning? I'm not sure I want to."

"Want's got nothing to do with it. This isn't anything compared to what the military nurses go through. You should see what they put up with before you start whining."

Both women quickly changed into their uniforms. Before she left, Mama had tucked her favorite cameo into Colleen's bra for protection. It was the one she had purchased from the estate sale of a Mrs. Martell, the one with the hugging ivory swans floating on a Celtic labyrinth. Colleen placed it in her bra now.

They joined five other nurses heading toward Nichols. Elizabeth quickly introduced them all. "Rita from Albuquerque, Rosemary from Michigan, Millie from Florida. Harriet left the paradise of San Francisco for Kentucky, and Ann is from Missouri, like me."

"You all left home to come serve the war effort?"

"You're not the only one with a good idea, Colleen. The rest of us figured out pretty early that first, we could do the job, and second, we'd become better nurses if we did. All of us want to do our part. There's nowhere else I'd rather be." Everyone agreed.

Elizabeth reported to the second floor where the ICU patients were housed. She spent the next twelve hours rotating from one to another, with barely a moment to look out a window and notice the grey skies accumulating in the west, or to feel the cold wind starting to whip up over the long, flat runways. She did not witness the planes rolling down the field, one after the other, flown by pilots preparing for combat.

Colleen reported to Nurse Anderson, who said, "Don't bother to clock in," and handed her a note. It read, "See me at once".

Colleen found Captain Chantel on the first floor, consulting with a doctor outside a patient's room. Her uniform was stained by the bloody fluids of a butchered soldier. Her face bore the worn-out expression of one who sleeps too little.

"O'Brien, right. I have a special assignment for you. I found out about it this morning. It's a little unorthodox, and it's not permanent, but for the next couple of months, you're going to teach at the School of Air Evacuation. We received orders to increase the number of graduates tenfold and need more instructors in the classrooms. Our injured soldiers trust us to bring them home. We are not going to let them down. You'll be the first link in the chain."

"I don't know anything about evacuating soldiers from a battlefield, what do I have to teach?"

"You're a good nurse, teach them that. Start class today to receive your training. Pay attention. When you finish, you'll be responsible for teaching groups of nurses who will graduate as second lieutenants. Only military nurses can fly on those planes. We're trying to get as many as we can in service as quickly as possible. You can't fly, but you can prepare those who will. What they learn here is important to the survival of their patients and themselves, O'Brien. See to it they are ready."

MISSION

Chapter Four

Leadership is the art of getting someone to do something you want done because he wants to do it.

GENERAL DWIGHT D. EISENHOWER

❊ ❊ ❊

Six weeks later, Colleen's relief that she had completed the course was exceeded by the fact that it went better than she supposed it would. It had been tough and challenging, but her brawn was sufficient to match the physical tests required. Those brisk walks around Cayuga Lake pushing Chloe in the carriage had paid off. Her doggedness rose from the brokenness she carried within and the need to blot out the painful truth of her shattered world, a world without Chloe.

The only thing that made the separation bearable was the commitment demanded by this mission and knowing it will bring them together when it is done. Intense and difficult manual labor, long hours that included classes, lectures, practice and study, along with constant pressure to drill, demonstrate ability, learn information and pass the exams took all her concentration. Perhaps under other circumstances, the pressure would not have been so terrible, but these were extraordinary times.

A war in the world, a war in my home. Life on both fronts has changed forever. I don't know how to fix either. All I do know is I will give every ounce of effort here, so I can reunite with my girl, my cherished girl. That will be my reward, she vowed, *that will be what I hold onto.*

At 0800, she reported to Nurse Nancy Martin, a no-nonsense woman with a determination to get our fighting men home, their healing jump-started. Standing on the tarmac covered with planes, she was all business in pursuit of her objective.

"Good morning, Nurse O'Brien. As you know, the medical officers, nurses and enlisted men ship out on our planes as soon as we graduate them. There is no opportunity for questions once they fly out of here, so make sure they are competent before you recommend them. I instruct the officers; Nurse Patton takes the enlisted men. You'll teach the nurses. Questions?"

"No, Nurse Martin."

"Class starts at 0900. Use this plane here for

practice. It will be open and available to you in the mornings and afternoons. Meet your students here. Use room 103 for instruction. Comprehend?"

"Yes, Ma'am, I do," she answered.

Colleen entered the heavy transport plane, an unarmed C-47 cargo, stripped down and parked near the base hospital. It was identical to the ones that carried troops home and would be her domain for demonstrating proper techniques. The women showed up singly, at first, then in small groups, quietly taking seats in chairs lined up by the entrance, rows one through four. Colleen tried to steady her trembling fingers. She felt intimidated facing this group of incredible women. *Settle down. Get a grip. Swallow.*

She called the roll in a clear and distinct voice, having practiced the names sitting in her bunk the night before, thirty-two women total. Their applications revealed that all of them were educated equal to, or better than, she. *What am I doing standing in front of them?* A few had acquired many hours of flight as former airline hostesses. *What can I teach them about flying?*

"Mary Francis, Catherine Duffy, Mae Olson, Martha Eldon, Gretchen Schmitt, Cora Schwartz," she read. Each name responded with a full feminine "yes". Somehow, their energy stiffened her spine. Recognizing that, she looked up to face them. *Deep breath. Repeat.* Nerves calmed, she held her shaking hands in closed fists by her side.

"Good morning."

"Good morning."

"I am Nurse Colleen O'Brien. I'm the instructor for nurses wanting to join the U.S. Army Air Force Air Evacuation Corps. Your job is to evacuate casualties as quickly as possible from combat zones. Your planes will be full of injured men. You are responsible for getting them to a base hospital, alive. In just a few weeks, you'll learn what would take a year elsewhere. It will be intense. We'll study the material and we'll practice. While this is new territory for all of us, everything we already know as nurses applies here. Is that clear?"

Some of the women stared at her, looked away or shifted uneasily in their chairs. One timidly raised her hand.

"I've been a pediatric nurse my whole career. Do you think what I know applies?" asked a striking brunette as thin as a runner. Mae Olson.

"If you're willing to apply yourself throughout the course, Nurse Olson, you will know what to do. Your instincts will kick in automatically. You'll get men to hospital treatment within an hour in most cases. Otherwise, it takes up to two weeks to transport them by rail or ship. We've evacuated 160,000 wounded in battle from the Solomon Islands to Africa. We've lost less than one per cent of them in flight."

Colleen studied their faces and saw several others struggling with fear and doubt, needing resolution. "Anyone else?" she asked with deliberate pause.

"I'm not concerned about the nursing part," another said, her voice growing stronger with each word. "I'm concerned about the military part. I don't know if I'm cut out for it. I'm a city girl. Have never left Philly. I may not be tough enough for the army." Second row, second seat. Emma Woodson, surgical nurse.

"Me, too. I've never been famous for my bravery. Now I'm going to be taking vitals on an airplane dodging fire from very big guns, trying to remember my place in the pecking order and how to salute," said Iris Davis, last row.

This is why I just love working with nurses. They're so thoughtful, compassionate, independent. How can I convince them they've got what it takes?

"A surgeon will command your flight if one is available. If not, you will command the flight. You will be in charge. Nurses are tough. You have more strength than you realize. You may be stretched to your limits, but you will know what to do."

"I ran the floor at St. Joe's in Detroit, where I'm from," continued Nurse Davis. "I'm not used to taking too many orders."

"You are in the military now, a member of the men's army. Learn military protocols. Show respect for the officers and enlisted. You may get less respect than you deserve, but you will know the good work that you do. Your resilience comes from within. While Army code may be stricter than what you're used to, it's not a lot different than the pecking order in a hospital. Your duty is to your country and your patients. If you remember that, you'll learn to accept the rest as part of the job."

"I've never been shot at before either. That terrifies me. Should it disqualify me, too?" Catherine Duffy, assistant to the famous orthopedic surgeon in Baltimore.

Colleen had spent the previous thirty-six days studying nonstop, wrestling with these same concerns, asking these same questions, struggling with the same self-doubt. This quest still terrified her, but she knew her sense of responsibility had grown and was formidable, her fear sublimated by a dependable commitment to the mission. It had come as a revelation that she, too, if called upon, could board a C-47 and meet the men on the ground. She was astonished by how competent she had become.

"It's the highest honor for me to be here, and you, too, ladies," said a woman who appeared older than the rest. Lily Thompson, cancer nurse, Lincoln Hospital in Wisconsin. "So many of our sisters are Rosie the Riveters, welding airplane parts or running machines in factories that make ball bearings. The greatest government in the world employs us in the greatest army in the world, the U. S. Army. We're going to defeat those damn Nazis and blow the Japs to smithereens."

"The generals will win the war, Nurse Thompson. We will win the day, when we bring our boys home, alive."

"My brother, Bill, he died at Pearl Harbor on the *USS Arizona*. He didn't stand a chance. We didn't get his body back. I'm anxious to get on that plane and do all I can to help our boys knock those devils off the face of the earth. Make them pay."

"Then you know how important it is that we do our jobs well, to save those guys who do have a chance," said Colleen. "Flying to free American soldiers trapped on the front means flying right into enemy fire. Your plane will be part of a squadron, usually consisting of five planes. One or two will be full of badly injured soldiers. The crews of the lighter planes in the squadron fly alongside you and proceed into range to draw the big guns, if necessary, to keep you safe. There are no guarantees, though. I will make sure you learn emergency procedures so you can handle whatever comes your way."

"Don't our planes carry the sign of the Red Cross? Won't that stop them from shooting us?" asked Jane Benton, school nurse.

"That's a bull's eye. It makes you a target. The enemy knows there are Americans on board and little defensive power. Heading out, you'll carry supplies and won't display the cross. There is no marking for non-combat status flights. Don't look to this for glory. Realize you enlisted for hard work, danger and risk."

Their unease registered in their faces.

"The best way to resist fear is to conquer it doing what you do best," Colleen said. "You're good nurses. After this course, you'll be better ones. Believe in that, not what frightens you."

The women looked at her, and each other, with a renewed sense of purpose. They were ready. Assured they were primed to begin, Colleen lined up the women beside the plane and began issuing commands.

"Those of you in forward positions will triage patients for evacuation. The extent of the patient's injuries establishes if air transport will harm him. I'll teach you what happens to the human body at various altitudes. Your priorities are to remove wounded soldiers from the battlefield, stabilize them, treat them however you can in flight, check vitals to keep them alive and transport them as quickly as possible into hospital care."

The nurses stood at attention, two by two, absorbing every word.

"Load the patient onto the gurney," she bellowed. "Immobilize the spine. Make sure your hands and arms are placed securely under his neck, shoulders and hips to fully support his weight."

The nurses did as instructed and maneuvered the volunteer patients onto stretchers.

"Now, lift the stretcher using the strength in your legs, not your back. Hold it using the full palms of your hands. Save fingers for delicate tasks. Your gloves will protect you from blisters and abrasions. Good. Walk forward into the plane and attach the stretcher to the hooks on the wall.

Start at the top, right side first, then left and continue down the row of hooks until all are loaded, four patients on each row. Belt them in securely. You don't want anyone rolling off."

Nurses heaved the first of twenty-four heavy litters onto the plane and clamped them tightly in place.

"Remember to attend to the patient during movement. Keep him steady, no jostling. Control his limbs and head. Proceed carefully but quickly. Complete loading as fast as you can. The enemy will be shooting at you. Efficiency is imperative."

Mae cried out in pain and wiped blood from her hand when she pinched her fingers between the metal hook and brackets. When she saw everyone looking at her, she quickly turned to support her patient, embarrassed by the fuss she'd made.

"You got that done in just under twenty minutes," Colleen said, when the last litter was loaded and snapped into place. "That's too long. Every minute you are on the ground, you are vulnerable. So are the guys you leave behind to fight. They'll do all they can to protect you, but you have to clear the injured ASAP, so the pilots can fly that plane out of there, and the guys on the ground can defend themselves. Repeat the whole thing, faster. Get the patients loaded in less than ten."

The nurses lifted the heavy stretchers and hauled them onto the plane once more. With each practice, they learned the best way to place the men on the stretchers, carry the stretchers into the plane's belly and attach them to the wall until they succeeded.

"Ten minutes. Excellent. I evaluated you on your loading techniques. You all did fine work. Enlisted men, some trained as medics, will fly with you, so supervise them and direct them to assist you. Triage and delegate to them accordingly. At each refueling stop, make rounds and check conditions, so you can outline the treatment necessary for the next leg of the trip."

Everyone smiled and eased up a little, assuming lunch break was near. They had practiced for four hours straight. Crankiness was setting in.

In a hospital or doctor's office, every nurse worth her salt knows who's got the best snack stashed in the back of her drawer, who has the memorable dark chocolate in fancy red foil. If that person also happens to be your friend, the two of you shared a delicious, even nourishing, supply throughout the day to add energy. Every nurse knew at least one friend like that back home. It's what got you through the day.

There were no stashes here, and no occasion to enjoy a bite if there were. Nurse O'Brien enforced a relentless schedule. Everyone was famished.

"You have to be equally efficient unloading the plane and getting your patients into an ambulance or hospital," she was saying. "We'll concentrate on that after lunch. The lives of these brave soldiers hinge on you, Nurse," she said, making eye contact with each. "They've gone through vicious, brutal combat. They are deeply wounded physically and, perhaps, emotionally, having seen and done violent things beyond anything we can imagine. Against all odds, they survived, their lives entrusted to you. Check their dog tags first thing, say their names. This may be your only encounter, but the hours you are responsible for that soldier are among his most important."

With that, they could barely wait to finish chow and return to practice. All afternoon they loaded and unloaded men and used every device in the plane until each action was fixed firmly in their muscle memory.

"Class is done for today," Colleen said, finally, to the exhausted group. "Tomorrow we'll start instruction in room 103 and discuss in-flight airway management and intubation, along with desert medicine and little-known tropical diseases, such as dengue fever. You will be tested on the material. To prepare, review the first three chapters in the manual. With Wednesday comes climate in the theater of operations and how to protect from the cold, treat frostbite and avoid snow blindness. Please review the outline. We'll tackle physiology, medical classification and record keeping in the coming weeks. Dosages differ at high altitude, so a meds review is necessary, as well as how to adjust transfusions. You will treat severe anemia and all sorts of trauma; head injuries, shock, coronary occlusions, sucking wounds of the chest. We'll review best practices for each and all forms of basic life support."

"Will we ever get to try out one of these big birds, just to see what it feels like?" asked Nurse Benton.

"Yes, of course. In one week, we'll board a plane. We need to know if any of you get air sickness. It's also a good time to grasp air routes, map reading and aircraft identification. When it comes to crash procedures, the pilots are experts, so take note and bring your gas masks for that session. You'll learn how to handle a parachute from the officers on base. To prevent drowning, you'll be fitted for your life jacket and receive swimming lessons at the Henry Clay Hotel pool, courtesy of the Red Cross. Carry the jacket with you on every flight."

"Parachutes and life jackets," said Nurse Duffy. "Oh, Lordy."

"You'll be so well trained you'll know how to use them and what to do," Colleen said. "We'll also practice our protocols from take-off at Bowman to final disposition of the patient in an ambulance or hospital. Your ability to supply a flight and arrange the logistics to run it successfully governs your right to graduate and serve as a Second Lieutenant Air Evac Nurse in the Army Air Corps."

With that, the women shouted out, "Right on!" and "Alleluia!" and "Bring it on!" unable to contain their eagerness.

She dismissed them and completed her plans for the next day before grabbing a quick dinner in the mess. Liz and the other three nurses she usually ate with, Rita, Millie and Harriet, weren't there, and she was in a hurry, not inclined to wait. She left without seeing them and catching up on their news.

Returning to the barracks by herself compounded the sense of aloneness that often steamrolled her, especially at night. She couldn't confide in her students and was too embarrassed for her colleagues to know the desperation she occasionally bore. *They are all so poised and secure.* She could have told colleagues at Cornell and missed the comfort that came from sharing intimate moments and private troubles with them. They would have understood and supported her, as they always did.

What a hypocrite I am, she thought, as she changed from her uniform into her pajamas. She sat on the bed and lifted the brush to her hair, stroking it slowly. *I tell my students to overcome their fear, as I have overcome mine these past six weeks. I could do what I ask them to do on a C-47. But I'm such a coward when it comes to Tommy. I'm scared as hell of him, of hurting Chloe, of being poor, ruining my reputation, making a mistake or falling apart. Who am I to preach courage when I am so full of dread?*

KINSHIP

Chapter Five

O sleep! O gentle sleep!
Nature's soft nurse.

WILIAM SHAKESPEARE

* * *

A week later, Elizabeth blew by her bunk with Liz's typical breezy manner. "Hey, Colleen, a bunch of us are going to Air Devils Inn," she interrupted. "Come and join us. They've got a wonderful beer garden. It's warm enough to sit outside tonight, if you wear a jacket."

"I've got some letters to write and I'm going to wash my undies, down to the last pair," Colleen replied.

"You should take some time off, O'Brien. A little break after this very hard day. You do know Kentucky has the best bourbon in the world, don't you? Most of it is made right around here."

"Another day, Liz, ok? I will check out this place you talk about so much, I will, another day."

"It's where all the best-looking pilots hang. Privates are off limits, they're still green, but the pilots are a blast. One of them might buy you a drink. Nothing like a hot flyer for a fun evening to wash away the gore. That's why we go!"

"You go, have fun. Tell me all about it over breakfast. I can do without a hot flyer. I'm getting a divorce, remember?" She cringed at the humiliation embroidered in that statement. It embarrassed her every instance she said it, so she rarely did. Liz, being Liz, had insisted on the full story, and she told her some of it. Not all. Not about the blow to the face. Not about the fear, the fury or the shame. Only if you live it can you know it.

Liz took that "no" for an answer and left in a swirl of noise and commotion as she gathered the rest of the tribe around her. The door slammed, leaving Colleen sitting alone with stationery on a book in her lap, tapping her pen. *What can I say to Mama and Papa? How do I explain everything that's happened? What can I say to Chloe?*

April 20, 1943

Dear Mama, Papa and Chloe, my beautiful girl,

I want you to know I miss you so much. And think about you every day, first thing in the morning and last thing at night. In between,

I am busy teaching air evacuation procedures. 32 students, everyone a volunteer. These flying Florence Nightingales are daring and highly skilled. They enlighten me as much as I do them, but the esteem is mutual. We complete our duties without issue. So far, so good. Every day is a new trial, but I know I serve a purpose here. No exertion is wasted. All our efforts added together will win this war. That may be the only thing that will. So please stay steadfast as we resist the forces invading our lives. These men and women do so every day. I am in awe of them.

I want to know all about you. Papa, are you exercising your knee like Doc Walton said you should? I know it hurts, but you must do it if you want to keep walking. Your joint requires a strong muscle to support it, so continue with your therapy. Otherwise, the arthritis will only grow worse.

Mama, I dream of eating dinner at your table, not that the food in the mess is awful, but it sure isn't your good cooking. Your brisket, your Sunday potatoes, your chocolate cake, my mouth waters thinking of it. I can't wait to taste them again.

But most of all, I miss my sweet girl, the sound of her giggle when she bathes, the smell of her when we snuggle, her baby kisses on my neck. I didn't know my heart could hurt so much and wonder why it must be so.

Please give her all the love you can. Tell her my name so she doesn't forget me. Mama, the picture you took of the two of us at the Statue of Liberty is my greatest treasure. The photo is brilliant, as usual. The textures, the view. It is a true reflection of my sweet girl's countenance and love. Her face, her smile, so full of light. Thank you for this gift, it's what keeps me going.

Kentucky is very different from New York. Sometimes I don't absorb what people say because of their accents or expressions, even though they speak English. The Louisvillians have been most kind to us. They always encourage us. I don't have much time to spend off base, but when I do, I meet the most interesting people. The locals are a mixture of horsemen, laborers, farmers, men who work on the river and women from the Appalachian Mountains. They display the hospitality of the South and seem to live peacefully with the Negroes, perhaps because the Negroes accept the imaginary line that divides black and white here, and most don't cross it.

The nursing crew come from all over the USA, each with an amazing story. I can't tell them now, but when I see you next, I will remember every one, don't you worry.

The air is clean, like Ithaca. The forests are tall and old, reminding me of those growing around the lake. Whenever I have an empty hour, I bike to the nearest park. There are some treasures here named after the Cherokee, Iroquois and Seneca tribes who came before. The scent of the emerging spring is in the air. It comes early in Louisville, oh joy, which makes me long for home even more. The wildflowers on Cornell's campus will be popping soon, I wish I could be there when they do.

I must say goodnight as I am too tired to write more. Please know you are always in my heart.

Hugs and kisses,

Your loving daughter,

Colleen

PS. Could you please send me a new picture of Chloe, Mama? Can I see how she's grown? I'd be very thankful.

Writing was never her strong suit, so she considered that the hardest part of the day. Relieved to be done with it, Colleen collected her underwear and a box of Ivory flakes, then went looking for the utility sink. *I miss my pretty undies, the pastels with the flowers and lace around the waist. When did I last feel feminine? Sexy? When did I last have sex? Sex I enjoyed?*

It hadn't been good with Tommy for a long while, ever since Chloe was born. It was as if he was jealous of the baby, but that is ridiculous. Fathers aren't jealous of their daughters, are they? His short fuse was hard to explain, though, especially after his blowups became first frequent, then physical.

Chores done, preparations complete for tomorrow, it was lights out. *What I would give for my own bed*, she thought, shifting to find a comfortable spot on her bunk, *my soft feather pillow and the log cabin quilt in blue, lavender and yellow that Mama sewed for me and Tommy.*

That bed. How she loved it. The feel of the rich cherry wood sanded and polished, the tall posts with simple carving, the clever bookshelf connecting them, the matching storage chest lined with cedar sitting at the end, just the right height to serve also as a cushioned bench. Tommy and Papa had conspired to build it without her knowing. They succeeded. The surprise and delight on her face the day of the wedding, when Tommy presented her with their handmade gift, said it all.

They celebrated together with pleasure on that happy day. How had loneliness become her chronic state of being since?

MELTDOWN

Chapter Six

The nurse of full-grown souls is solitude.

JAMES RUSSELL LOWELL

❊ ❊ ❊

"I'm concerned about you, O'Brien. It's Saturday night. Let's get out of here and destress. Come on, you're coming with me, the Devils await."

"Not tonight, Liz. I'm just not up to it. I've got to tidy up for inspection tomorrow."

"That's what you said last night. You've not taken a break since you got here. You'll crack up if you don't, trust me, and I don't want you to lose it. Your room is perfect, and you're worried about passing inspection? Spend a couple of hours with your dancing shoes on. Have a laugh. Don't keep our friends waiting for you, Ann and Millie are at the door."

When Elizabeth insists, she is hard to deny. Colleen wanted to complete her nightly ritual and slink into her corner, but instead she grabbed her purse and stuffed her sleeves into the black velvet jacket that stood out for being perfect for a lovely dinner at Malone's and completely inappropriate at an airfield.

The small group of nurses walked to the Air Devils Inn and entered the hometown watering hole that catered to the men and women of Bowman Field. Photographs and signs covered the walls. Flashing yellow or red lights spelled out advertisements for Schlitz or Falls City beer. Full ashtrays sat in the center of every Formica-topped table. The black leather tufted chairs, striped with duct tape, showed the wear and tear of thousands of bodies resting and rocking on their seats. Unfiltered Camel cigarette smoke colored the air gray, causing her eyes to burn and lungs to gag on the odor, but the place was lively and full of fun. Everyone was living this moment fully, not thinking of the dreaded tomorrow.

"Come on, let's grab this booth," Liz said, as their shoes scuffed the sticky floor. "They're hard to come by."

"We can leave our coats here," Millie said. "Our stuff will be ok, it's a friendly crowd."

"Yeah, most everybody knows somebody, so the party never stops and always changes as the guys come and go. If you don't know anybody now, Colleen, you will soon," Ann shouted over the sound of the blaring jukebox.

Just then, four guys approached them, all dressed in their military flight jackets and smiles as wide as their faces. The women moved into a half circle around the booth, Colleen in the middle. The men crowded in on both sides. There was no chance Colleen was going home early.

Will Shumer, a pilot who looked like he should be planning his date for the high school prom, with fuzz, not whiskers, for his mustache, insisted on buying the first round. Everyone declared a toast. "Here's to lady luck," Will began, gulping his beer, and the others joined him.

"Here's to killing Japs and obliterating Germans!" Max Thomas shouted. They all cheered with drinks held high, glasses clinking in midair.

"I'll drink to flying my B-17 over Tokyo and Berlin to drop bombs directly on Hirohito's and Hitler's head," called out Fred Haley.

"Cheers," they yelled, louder, pounding their fists on the table, followed by big swigs.

"This is for my lady back in Texas, Jenny Welch," said a handsome guy with sparkling green eyes sitting on the end. This was Jeff Winters, the last guy you'd expect to be sentimental, with all that muscle and the stoic look on his face. "She's the prettiest, smartest gal in the world and sweeter than baby's breath. I'm going to make her my bride the day I get back to Dallas."

Max slapped the back of his friend's head and

threw his cap in the air. Everyone roared loudly and another round was due.

"What about you, ladies, what do you want to drink to?" asked Will after the second drinks were served.

One by one they responded. "I drink to the best damn nurses in the world," Millie squealed over the crowd.

"Hell yes!" came the reply. The guys banged their glasses on the table and stomped their feet.

"I'm thinking of all the fellows I've treated at Nichols. They're the heroes. They are survivors. Cheers to them," Ann said. The gaggle went wild and songs broke out, full verses of *Praise the Lord and Pass the Ammunition.*

"Alright, lovely lady, it's your turn," Will said to Colleen. "What do you want to drink to?"

"Oh, Will, nothing, I've got nothing," she pleaded. Her brain went blank. She blushed every shade of red.

He eyed her name tag. "Come on, Nurse O'Brien, there must be a guy back home, or maybe a man on the front, who rates a beer in his honor. Which is it, O'Brien?"

She felt her tongue twist into a stammering knot.

"A pretty little thing like you must have one or the other," Will insisted.

Colleen couldn't think of a response, and for no reason she could explain to them, she burst into tears in a profusion of sobs and gulps. Too choked to suck air into her lungs, it was difficult to breathe. Everyone at the table paused, stared and did not move again, until Elizabeth threw an arm around Colleen's shoulder to calm her.

"Come on, O'Brien, perk up. Drink your beer. Look around you, girlfriend, this is a celebration." Liz gave her a firm hug, then let go.

Colleen straightened herself and wiped the tears. She fished in her pockets for a hanky and caught her runny nose just before it dripped. She reeked of embarrassment, unable to look them in the eye. These were the first tears she'd shed since the long bus ride to Louisville, and they fell here, in front of strangers at a bar. Except, she realized in her fog, they weren't strangers. They were friends. They were family. They were all in this together.

"Hey, Colleen, no one meant any harm. I'd as soon bite a bug as see you hurting. Why don't I walk you back to the barracks, ok?" It was Jeff, and his kindness touched her.

"I'm fine, Jeff, everyone, really. I don't know what came over me. Just missing home, I guess, but I think I will turn in. I don't want to spoil a good time for all of you. I can walk it alone."

"No way, Nurse O'Brien, will the men of this air base let a lady walk back by herself. What would the brass think of us if we were such cads? Grab your coat. I'll have you home in fifteen minutes."

Goodbyes were quick. Jeff placed her hand in the crook of his strong arm, guiding her carefully down the street, protected, cared for and valued. It had been a while since a man held her close and secure.

At the door, she said shyly, "Thank you, Jeff, I appreciate you walking me here."

"My pleasure, Nurse O'Brien. I hope we can meet another day under happier circumstances. Your sadness tonight would make a glass eye cry." A faint smile creased the dimples in his cheeks.

"I hope so, too. I'll see you at the Devils. I assume they'll let me in again after the scene I made."

"My orders are to fly out tomorrow, Colleen, reporting for duty in Europe. Don't know where exactly yet. Leave the important decisions to the Army, right?"

"Oh, Jeff, this was your last evening at Bowman? I'm sorry I ruined your night out."

"Impossible, ma'am. It was my pleasure. You be good, you hear?"

"Take care of yourself, Jeff," she said, extending her hand to shake.

He lifted it and gave it a sweet kiss. "I'm good to go. This is why I joined up. I want to get it over with. The sooner I do, the sooner I see Jen. I'll do whatever it takes to get back to her."

With that they hugged, a quiet moment between two souls connecting in the night, no Jen, no Tommy, in sight.

STORY

Chapter Seven

*Never waste a minute thinking
about people you don't like.*

GENERAL DWIGHT D. EISENHOWER

❋ ❋ ❋

It was a relief to cry it out, but the combination of alcohol, tears and the weariness of grueling days caused Colleen to fall into a fitful sleep that night, the least amount of rest she'd had since leaving Ithaca.

Sunday morning, Elizabeth was standing beside her bed, first thing. "Get up," she said. "We're going out in some of this bright Kentucky sunshine to take a walk in the park and let the fresh air sober us."

Colleen rolled on her side and opened her eyes to look at her friend. The last thing she wanted was a walk in the park. The hangover might kill her.

"Liz, no, I can't. I made a fool of myself last night. I'm going to hide under these covers until I have to show my face Monday at drill."

"Look, Colleen, no one cares about last night. I'm not joking around. I'm concerned about your mental health. You've been forlorn, shall we say, since I met you. I see how you hide out in your corner, never playing with the rest of us. You burst out crying in the middle of a party at the Devils among some of the handsomest guys in the USA. What gives?"

Colleen pulled the blanket over her head. "Please, don't remind me. I'm so embarrassed."

"I don't care that you're embarrassed. I care that you broke down. Something must be going on with you. Whatever it is, you gotta snap out of it. You won't make it, if you don't. We must be strong. We can't afford a weak link. Consider this required counseling. Get on your feet, throw on this pair of pants and let's go figure out what's up."

As always, Liz was difficult to ignore. Reluctantly, Colleen pulled on the pants, lifted the old sweatshirt from the back of her only chair and zipped the front. She tied her normally shiny, smooth, shoulder-length bob into a ponytail, then lowered the brim of her NY Yankees baseball cap to shelter her eyes from the bright light. Her casual appearance provided enough disguise that her recruits would not recognize her. For them she dressed impeccably, professionally. None of them had seen last night's melt down, a grace that saved her.

The two women headed in the direction of Seneca Park, where they wandered aimlessly along the path, getting in the groove. Liz possessed that quality inherent in so many nurses; she exuded genuine concern, so that even someone with secrets as deep as Colleen's knew it was ok to share them.

Colleen had spoken no more than necessary to do her job while waiting for her jaw, and her spirit, to heal, making her seem introverted, aloof, perhaps. In her shell-shocked state, she hadn't connected closely with these nurses, like she had with those in Cornell's obstetrics department. There, they spent twelve-hour shifts telling their stories while making sure a host of infant souls saw their first daylight. Here, she was thinking, *it's best to reveal as little as possible, until I get the lay of the land. Figure out what's happening, what I'm dealing with, how I'm going to make it.* Her mantra remained, *keep going, stay alert, do what I can until something makes sense.* Colleen's reticence had interfered with making meaningful relationships with these women, who were now her colleagues. No wonder she lived in loneliness.

Liz was the only nurse with whom she personally engaged, mainly because that's what Liz did, engage. Colleen didn't know that much about her, but she appreciated that Liz cared. They didn't work together, only exchanged hellos in the showers, and some days a meal, if they happened to be in the mess at the same hour. A few times Colleen had stopped by Liz's bunk to join the crowd, those who dropped in for a chat then stayed all evening. She enjoyed Liz's welcome, but when shyness overcame her, she quickly left.

It seemed like forever since Colleen had talked to anyone. It was no longer possible to visit with Mama or Sarah about anything, not long distance. Even conversations that are short and to the point, like the days when both she and Sarah were busy with jobs, kids and household chores, seemed off limits when there was no time or telephone. *Where would I begin to tell Sis the story? What does she know? Did Mama talk to her? What must she think of me? And Tommy? What would I tell her about Tommy? What should I tell Liz about Tommy?*

"So, what is the pickle you're in, and how do we get you out of it?" Liz began, as they strolled the perimeter of the park. Short and to the point, a good start. She directed Colleen to a bench. They both took a seat under a tree as fine-looking as any in New York.

"In February, I was Tommy O'Brien's wife and mother to Chloe, sipping iced tea while bread baked in my oven on a Saturday morning. Chloe was fighting a bad cold. She played by my side, games like Peek a Boo and Where Am I. She loved them all, and I loved making her laugh with silly faces and goofy voices. It was a happy day! Then on Sunday afternoon, Tommy slugged me. It was the second time, and all was lost. I can't get over it, or figure out what happened, where it all went."

"Where do you think it went?"

"Down a deep, ugly hole of unbearable ruin."

"Woah! Before we throw your life into the abyss, would it help to start at the beginning?"

"In the beginning, we married too young, when I was eighteen, right out of school, and quickly got pregnant with Chloe. I'd be lying if I said I was thrilled. I feared a pregnancy would get in the way of my dream of becoming a nurse. But I wanted to make it work and enrolled in nursing school, the advanced course. During months of morning sickness, a full-blown pregnancy and then childbirth, I studied my butt off to complete my classwork and clinicals. I graduated with a baby on my hip and passed my state exam the next month."

"The world is a better place because you did."

"Once I met my sweet Chloe, I knew she was a godsend, and I was the happiest mom in the world. We lived in a tiny home with a roof that leaked and struggled with too much to do and not enough money, plus a baby with lots of respiratory issues, but I thought we were happy. Mama and Papa stood by us, and my sister, Sarah, helped when she could. Chloe thrived with all the people who loved her. The day I graduated was one of my proudest. Everyone was there for the grand event. I thought we had it made, things were going to get easier. Mr. and Mrs. O'Brien were on their way, eager to have a second child, if one came along."

"How did this idyllic scene become an unbearable ruin?"

"That's what I'm trying to figure out. My job at Cornell suited me just fine. The pay was ok, hours were sufficient, and, best of all, the staff was terrific and taught me much. They gave me faith in myself that I could do this, could be good at it even. It meant everything to have them affirm this is my calling."

"That's ideal. I still don't see the problem."

"Well, the more I thrived, the surer I grew, and the more negative Tommy became. He criticized my cooking, made fun of my hair, said I looked like a nun when I knotted it into a bun to tuck under my cap. He complained when I studied, refused to watch Chloe when I was preparing for exams, resented me going to school. He put his dirty feet on my whites if I lay my uniform on the bed. He rolled his eyes and laughed at me when I spoke. If I complained, he said I was too emotional, told me to stop acting hysterically."

"My older, smartass brother used to do that eye rolling thing. It would send me over the edge. I am completely intolerant of it."

"I couldn't do anything right and spent considerable effort trying to keep him happy. I gave up talking about the people I saw every day and what happened to them, my best friends. It became easier to avoid the subject than discuss what interested me."

"Sounds like a guy who couldn't stand seeing his wife succeed. That problem is in his head, not yours."

"My great ambition was to love Tommy O'Brien. We've been together since we were kids. I've never looked at another guy."

"Maybe that's the real issue. Maybe you should have. And, hon, this is the perfect place to find out. It's full of men, eighteen hundred to be exact, and they're all as fine as a frog's hair split four ways, as my grandma used to say."

"I can't look at another man, Liz. I'm beating with a broken heart. I gave up so much to come here. I miss my daughter."

"You are here to become a better nurse. You are here to serve your country, right?"

"I have become a better nurse. I am committed to this mission."

"Then you are much better off than you were two months ago. Chloe is where she belongs, receiving the love of her grandparents. You no longer live with a man who thinks it's ok to smack you. You're earning stars for Clara Barton's heavenly crown. Maybe it's your chance to kneel and kiss the ground. Seems to me you've got all you need, more than what you asked for. Don't you think that's sufficient to take care of yourself?"

"I want to be with Chloe."

"You will be."

"I want her to have an education."

"She will have."

"I want to give her a full life, not a half one."

"You will give Chloe all you can, that will be enough."

"I can't count on Tommy anymore. I sure as hell will not beg him to take care of us."

"You think he won't?"

"I don't know what he'll do. I didn't think he'd hit me. I didn't think Chloe would watch me get knocked out on the floor. When I came to, Tommy stood there with his fists clenched, Chloe sprawled on top of me, crying, so petrified. I'll never forgive myself for putting her through that."

"Heavens to Betsy, there's a tree stump in Mississippi thinking more clearly than you are. That makes no sense, ya' know? You didn't put her through that, Colleen, Tommy did, when he planted that black eye on you. The question is, do you want her to witness another one? You caught a break at Bowman. Be glad for a second chance. Be glad Chloe will never again see his fingerprints on your face. Never again see you as a victim."

"I'm not a victim. I've never been a victim."

"Exactly. Don't become one in Tommy O'Brien's hands. You're a competent nurse, Colleen, and I can only imagine how much you miss mothering. But you made the right decision to come here. You're sun-kissed to be rid of a man who sees nothing wrong with thumping his wife. If he hit you once, if he hit you twice, he'll likely hit you a third and a fourth time. When will you make him stop, if not now? Do you have the brains God gave a goose? Or do you like being pummeled?"

"I want him to stop. I want to create a new life for us. That's why I came to Louisville to join the air evacuation school."

"And now you are trained and fully qualified to teach in that same school. Oh, how the world turns. If you were right to come here, and you were, why do you beat yourself up for succeeding? If you want to make a life for yourself and Chloe, what's stopping you?"

"Nothing, I suppose, it's just that I never wanted a divorce. I wanted a marriage that was as full of love as Mama and Papa's. Fifty years. We didn't make it to five."

"No one wants a divorce, but that's not the point. You have to play the cards you're dealt, Colleen, but the cards you're holding shouldn't include a husband who beats you."

"I'm so saddened by all I've lost. My marriage, my cozy home, my family and my colleagues at Cornell. Most of all, my daughter. I'm starting over and worried to death. I don't know what's going to happen next, or what to believe."

Liz let out one of her trademark laughs, recognizable by anyone who heard it once. "Lordy, girl, join the club. Everyone feels that way. We're all starting over and worried to death. None of us knows what will happen next. We're all in the same soup. Why do you think you're special? Why should you have all the answers?"

"I don't think I'm special. I don't know what I

am. I've never been like this before."

"Bless your pea pickin' heart. None of us have, friend, none of us have. Forget about Tommy O'Brien for now. When this is over, and you return to Ithaca, use what you learn here to find a job that pays enough for you and Chloe. You will make it on your own, Colleen, if that's what you want to do. You and Chloe will be just fine."

"How do I get used to the shame over such a failure?"

"By growing from it. Failure has the power to teach you some valuable lessons. Decide what they are and learn them."

"I'm so angry at him for hurting me."

"Good. You should be. Stay pissed off. The anger will keep you moving."

"Until I spent that night on the bus to Louisville, I'd never been alone. I don't ever want to feel that lonely again."

"You won't, darlin', you're one of us now."

"I never expected it to be like this."

"No one expected it to be like this. It's not about what we expect, Nurse O'Brien. It's about what life expects from us."

"I've never asked why you're here, Liz. What brings you to Louisville?"

"Some of the same things that brought you, except I also need to find my husband, Van. We spent our six-day honeymoon at Lake of the Ozarks more than a year ago. That was the last I saw him, December 18, 1941. He's been missing in action since stationed in the Pacific. I'm here to track him down."

"Oh, Liz, no, how awful."

"It is hell. One of his buddies told me he was burned in an explosion when Japan attacked them. Bandages on both his hands. Then he disappeared. Van earned more than two thousand hours flying for Western Airlines before the war. I wonder if he'll be able to use his hands to fly another plane. I wonder if he's alive."

"Liz, you never said anything. I didn't know."

"I don't like to talk about it. Everyone treats me with kid gloves, when they find out. I don't want special recognition. I want to earn respect based on merit, not pity."

"You must feel as lonesome as I do, yet you put on such a brave front."

"All of us have lost someone or something, Colleen. We're all testing our mettle to triumph over fear. We put on a brave front just to get through the day. I don't know of any other way, do you?"

"No, I don't."

"The world breaks around us, one day after another. The silver lining is, you and I have the ability to help mend it. Never has there been a greater challenge, or a greater need. Do your job, Colleen, do it well. Allow the rest to fix itself. Things will settle down eventually. We both must live for that."

PREPARATIONS

Chapter Eight

Life is a lively process of becoming.

GENERAL DOUGLAS MACARTHUR

❋ ❋ ❋

"O'Brien, come quick! Chantel's knickers are in a knot," Liz shouted the length of the barrack's hallway.

"What are you saying? Nothing rattles Chantel," said Colleen, poking her head around her privacy wall built from a stack of luggage.

"Something did. She's called us back to the hospital pronto. Get your gear on."

"I've been running all over hell's half acre today and I'm plum tuckered out. I can't take one more step."

"Hey, you sound like a southerner, stay a little longer and the governor will make you a Kentucky Colonel. But Chantel's orders are not optional. Get your butt up and let's go find out what the snafu of the day is."

When they arrived at Nichols, a line of nurses and other staff stood assembled before the Chief Nurse. "Thank you for showing up after hours," she began. "My orders to you tonight come from Commander Jolson. His wife, and other members of the Officers' Wives Club, will host a Derby Day party. While our attendance is not mandatory, we are the special guests and, if not on duty, should consider the invitation carefully.

"The event will be held in one week, Saturday, May 1, in the Roof Garden at the Brown Hotel. Drinks and appetizers included. The Bowman Bombardiers will provide music for dancing. Sign up by Wednesday. Buses will drive you to the Brown. That's it, as you were."

The group dismissed. Colleen and the other women returned to the barracks. "The Commander's wife, is she the one we saw touring in the high falutin' convertible?" Millie asked as they walked.

"Yup, that's the one," said Liz.

"Remember when she and some other white-gloved ladies held a picnic under the maple tree on the west side of the building? The day the first full plane of injured soldiers arrived. In the middle of that bedlam, they looked so out of place with their tiny sandwiches and fluted glasses, blood spurting to the clouds not thirty feet away."

"She might be a little clueless," Liz said.

"She's a snob," said Rita. "She held her nose so high in the air, she would have drowned if it rained. I'm not going to some fancy pants party for her."

"Oh, yes you are. We all are. This will be the biggest thing that happens at Bowman all year."

"I can't afford a party dress," said Colleen.

"Normally, I'd agree with you, but not today. You don't want to be the only one wearing a shirtwaist. We'll find a nice little summer frock on sale and add some accessories. You'll be gussied up like Cinderella going to the ball when I'm finished."

"Thanks, Liz, my fashion consultant. What would I do without you?"

"Or I you? It works both ways, doll, don't you get that?"

To the group she said, "Just you wait until we get to the party and see all the festivities. You'll be glad you went. We'll have a chance to dance the steps we practiced at the USO."

"The only fella' I want to dance with is my Ben," complained Harriet, "and he won't be there."

"Listen up, Harriet, everyone," said Liz. "This is not about you. The officers' wives like to put this shindig on for us. They spend quite a few ration stamps to pay for it. Don't insult them by staying home. It makes Chantel look good when her nurses show up, and we want her to look good. She does plenty for us. So, sign up, ladies. Do your bit."

Liz made a valid point. Captain Chantel was a truly humble woman, interested in the well-being of her patients and staff, who felt her presence even when she was not there. Her authority came from that, and no, Colleen did not want to let her down. She would do her bit.

The evening before the dance, Colleen and Liz strolled down Frankfort Avenue, window shopping for items on sale. Posters advertising investments in war bonds hung from light poles. Red, white and blue flags draped every window.

They crossed side streets where housewives stood in their backyards, hanging laundry and talking over fences with their neighbors. Some of the shops had closed, but the pharmacy, which sold soap, remained open. Liz and Colleen entered through the door and heard the bell above it ring.

Liz rummaged through her large purse as they wandered the aisles; lipstick, powder, streetcar tokens, $2.00 in cash, a leather notebook with her initials EAK. "Got any chewing gum?" she asked.

Colleen searched hers and came up empty. When did she ever spend her paycheck on anything frivolous?

"How about cigs, got any of those?"

"I don't have the habit, never started."

"Guess I should buy both, then. Wonder what's new on the ration list this week."

"Meat, coffee, butter, cooking fat, gas and shoes, due to a leather shortage. Your cigs are safe."

"At least there is still some pleasure in this girl's life. Lord knows, I don't ask for much."

Liz paid for her items while Colleen gathered her supplies. On a top shelf, she noticed a can of "Old Spice", the shaving cream Tommy kept on the back of the bathroom sink.

She liked to watch him shave, when he was unaware and naked except for a towel around his waist; cocky and sure, wet curls in black hair, water drops drying on his clean-smelling shoulders. With a brush he'd lather his heavy beard using water and soap, rinse to soften, then apply the shaving cream. Pulling a Gillette Safety Razor blade downward over tight skin, cheeks first, ears to chin, he would sometimes sing a favorite song and sway his hips. The last time she watched, she leaned with her back on the wall, unseen behind the door, Chloe napping in her arms, and saw his sexy reflection in the mirror. She hummed along with him, bearing witness to a life fulfilled. That was eleven days before he hit her the first time.

An involuntary shudder shook her core. To release the memory, Colleen grabbed any soap she could find and bought two bars, one for her, one for Liz. They exited the store and joined the crowd heading west. It was getting late, and Louisville grew lively on a Friday night. Crowded streets carried hundreds of people walking to their favorite restaurants, theaters or bars. Everyone reveled in the cheerful atmosphere.

Colleen and Liz hopped onto the trolley to ride down the main drag, passing bright lights and honking horns, crowds shuffling and storefront barkers plying their trade. A parade of happy people, as lively as those on their way to a Broadway play, walked by.

They exited the trolley at the third stop and joined the walkers. The women wearing clipped hair bobs and pants were the envy of those not yet so daring, including Liz and Colleen, whose skirts swirled in the breeze. Those slacks looked comfortable and enabled the wearers the freedom to move without caution. Plus, the women stuffed useful pockets with items like dollar bills and a handkerchief. Colleen noticed style, color and fabric and pictured the first pair she would sew; black, designed so the legs tapered to the ankle, in a functional material like gaberdine. Those whose slacks fit well looked sleek and stylish, strong yet feminine, like Katherine Hepburn. Colleen couldn't wait to have the money to splurge.

The evening grew cool, so they flagged a Yellow Cab to drive them to Market Street, where they looked at the mannequins in Bacon's Department Store window. Deciding to take a chance, they entered the revolving doors. On the first floor, racks full of fine millinery, wrapped in ribbons and stuffed with feathers, waited for devotees of horse racing to make a last-minute selection that would enhance their sensational Derby Day costumes. Satin slips, excellent looking foundation garments, Sunday dresses and Victory Garden denims for $2.79 (*Oh! They would be fabulous to wear.)* filled the second floor. From the third-floor stairs, they entered a pathway of party dresses draped on every hanger; red, yellow, green and blue, every color in the rainbow.

They got busy. Liz decided on a bright red floor-length gown. She looked stunning in it. Colleen tried on a plain pastel blue dress in soft chiffon with a pretty lace collar and long sleeves. She was pleased with, and surprised by, the fit around her waist. Marching in drills had slimmed her down to pre-baby weight. She liked bearing a lighter load.

"Carry my small, white handbag," said Liz, "and wear the shiny black shoes with the solid heels that never leave your trunk. The bows on the toes dress them up. I'll loan you some jewelry, you'll look like a princess."

"Thanks, Liz, it's a good price," Colleen said, checking the tag. "I can do this," It felt good to buy something that pretty, she realized, folding the dress over her arm. "How about you?"

"I'm all set. After we pay, let's trade in our war stamps at the victory booth on the first floor," she said, heading for the door. "Do you have more coupons in your book?"

"I have extras with the ones Papa slipped into his letters."

"That's a nice Papa to share with you."

"He is nice. Papa swore the day I was born we would have our picture taken together every year, and we always have. Mama took the photos with the same Brownie, which she bought for $10.00 in

1915. Twice she lost it, then found it, once it was broken, but she fixed it before my birthday. Here is the first one," Colleen said, pulling two photos from a pocket in her purse. "The baby is me. This one shows the two of us at Coney Island, when I was sixteen."

"You kept growing, your Papa stayed the same."

"He never changes. He's always been a good Papa."

"A lot of fathers make commitments like that. A lot don't follow through. Yours did."

"That's the kind of man he is."

"The apple didn't fall far from the tree."

"What's your Papa like, Liz? Are you close to him?"

"Oh, no, I ran as far from the tree as I could get. My Pa wasn't around much, always out looking for day labor, could never hold a job long. When he found one, he spent what he earned on liquor."

"That must have been tough on you."

"It was. We lived in a small town then, in a state of shame. Everyone knew our business. Our old house sat on the edge of town, more shabby shack than cozy cottage. We were too poor to paint, too vain to whitewash. That has yet to change."

"I've never known poverty like that. Did it scare you?"

"We didn't know any different, always lived on the fringe, with never enough extra for school events or holidays. My brothers, sisters and I wore hand-me-down clothes from the local church 'seconds' bin. The other kids knew it, would laugh at us in class when we showed up wearing their old stuff. Many days a bowl of rice and beans is what we ate because there was nothing else. Many days we went to bed hungry because the rice and beans ran out. More than once, the mice got to them first. Ma worried herself silly, but she wouldn't ask for help."

"How did you get from there to here?"

"Science was my way out. Mr. Fowler saw my interest in it. He encouraged me to stay after school and take advantage of an empty lab. I learned so much exploring during those uninterrupted hours, trying things out, never getting bored. I found a life there and never looked back. It was the perfect escape from the drafty walls and furry, wild critters scurrying around the room I shared with my two sisters."

"Thank heavens for Mr. Fowler."

"Yep, I wouldn't be here without him. Science led me directly to nursing as a practical way to earn a living. Turns out, I've got the touch. Nursing has been my salvation. It's given me a chance to live the life I want. I haven't eaten red beans since. I'm glad every minute I wear my uniform. My profession is the one thing no one can take from me, the one thing that has never failed me. I will always be a nurse."

DERBY

Chapter Nine

We have learned to be citizens of the world, members of the human community.

PRESIDENT FRANKLIN D. ROOSEVELT

* * *

It was a splendid Kentucky Derby that first Saturday in May. Clear blue skies shined overhead as the temperamental three-year-old thoroughbred, Count Fleet, ridden by a jockey dressed in yellow silks, easily surpassed his rivals by three lengths. Ladies in the grandstand at Churchill Downs posed wearing dazzling, spring hats full of roses and bows. Refreshing mint juleps chilled the palms of every willing hand.

Nurses on duty at Nichols were unable to cheer for their favorite horse, running to win the most exciting two-minute race in sports. Instead, they wore starched, white caps for their chapeaus and were too busy tending to the muddled misery of the maimed to notice. But when their shifts concluded, their laughter floated through the barracks. They rushed to change into party clothes, everyone in a good mood, happy to leave the cruelty of the day behind.

Liz poked her head around the corner. "Do you have any nail polish? Mine is hard as a rock."

"Mama sent a care package that arrived today with some cookies she baked and Revlon's newest color, Mrs. Miniver Rose," Colleen said.

"Let me taste one of those cookies and give me some Mrs. Miniver, please. I would like rose toes showing from the tips of my shoes tonight. They'll match my outfit."

"Naturally. Cookies are in the box on the shelf. I'll trade you Mrs. Miniver for some hair barrettes."

"Here you go, doll," Liz said, taking two barrettes from her head and exchanging them for the polish. "How are you wearing your hair tonight?"

"Well, I'm not putting it in a bun," Colleen said. In high school, her Veronica Lake style looked as good as any, because her hair was thick and long. In uniform, she wore it pulled from her face and hidden under her cap. Tonight she brushed it to hang loose on her shoulders. It fell into a smooth and shiny pageboy that framed her oval-shaped face and large, dark eyes. The light rouge blended in her skin, and the pink lipstick sparkled from

76

her generous lips. Liz clasped a necklace under her collar that complemented the pastel dress, and her artful outfit looked both coordinated and flattering.

"You look great just as you are, don't touch a thing," Liz said.

"Think so?" Colleen questioned. "I'm not wearing a gorgeous gown like you."

"If you really want to sparkle and look a little less like a schoolgirl, you could put something in your hair, like a headband of flowers. Rita has one, ask if you can borrow it. Here, use this eyebrow pencil to draw a line up the back of your legs and pretend you're wearing stockings. We're going to a party! Ship sails at seven."

Nurses, doctors, staff, enlisted men and officers from every department of the hospital and base boarded the bus for the Brown Hotel with a middle-aged woman at the wheel. A few of the fellows made jokes about female drivers, which she ignored as she skillfully drove them to their destination.

The setting was like nothing Colleen had ever seen, as extravagant as the New Year's Eve Cotillion she attended every year with her parents at Madison Square Garden. In the ballroom, opulent baskets of floral bouquets stood poised on pedestals lining the walls and hung from the white ceiling with gold stars painted in the dome. Flaming candles cast soft light. Marble floors glistened. Purple velvet draped tall windows. Music emanated from a grand piano and orchestra on a central stage decorated in a spring garden motif. Impressive patriotic settings, designed as moving tributes to our war heroes, led to the roof and blended into the natural milieu. A brilliant whole moon glowed in a navy-blue night sky.

"Look at this," said Liz, after their jackets were checked and they settled with a drink at an empty table. "White cloth napkins, shrimp on skewers with cocktail sauce, fancy crackers, strolling violinists and waiters who want to serve us champagne. Oooh, la la, I have never lived so well."

"I must admit, I'm surprised. Who knew Kentuckians could throw a fancy soiree like this?"

"Let's not waste the evening. We'll hit the buffet table first and get a taste of everything. Then we'll circulate."

"You act like you've been to one of these before."

"I have, and I'm a girl who learned well how to have fun. Follow me, follow an expert."

Colleen stood and turned from her chair, heading for the food. "Wait," said Liz, grabbing her arm with one hand and holding up a flask with the other. "Before we mingle, let's spike our punch with this, the best bourbon for the best show in town." She added a shot to each glass, they toasted with a sip and headed in the direction of a table loaded with fresh fish, sparkling fruit, several kinds of bread, a variety of cheeses and crisp vegetables rolled in delicate, thin crusts, oozing honey sauce with every bite.

The large round table held three types of dessert: fresh baked blackberry pie, homemade ice cream and a sumptuous carrot-cinnamon cake with real cream-cheese frosting. All this was embellished by the soft radiance of happy guests talking to each other. They recognized this event was first class and expressed gratitude.

Muscular men and women in swirling skirts blocked their path, dancing the jitterbug with no inhibitions. Colleen admired their style, the swinging and twirling. She envied their ability to feel the music and express energy in every muscle in their bodies through rhythmic, jubilant movement. *Have I ever been that uninhibited? That carefree? Have I ever reveled that much over anything? I want to be a part of that! I want to let go, to be so liberated that I can cut loose on the dance floor and not think for a minute about how silly I might look.*

Before they emptied their plates, Liz's dance card was full. One after another of these excellent young men walked toward her, made small talk, asked to sign her card and kindly made way for the next one in line.

Colleen's card, on the other hand, bore no signatures. "You have to loosen up a little, Colleen," Liz advised. "If I were a guy, I wouldn't come near you either."

"Am I that bad?"

Liz deftly lifted the miniature fork to place the last tiny fruit-tart in her mouth. "You're not bad at all. You're lovely, but your body language says everything. The air you give off shouts 'leave me alone', so they do. If you want to party tonight, try to act like you're enjoying yourself. Who knows, maybe you will."

"I don't mean to give off an air, it's just that everything is so awkward. I'm still a married woman and have to act like one. It would be wrong to lead them on."

"Good Lord, Colleen, I'm a married woman and I'm not leading them on. You won't either. You're dancing, that's it. No one will ask you to get married tonight."

"But isn't it unfair of me to hide that from them?"

"You're not hiding anything from them. They want to dance with a pretty girl and forget what they will do tomorrow. We want to enjoy their company and forget what we had to do today. We all want to act like peace is possible. Perhaps that's how we help bring it about, by believing it is possible. That's how we stay sane, by dancing as if it's the sensible thing to do."

"If they knew I had a husband, they would not be interested in me."

"If they knew, they would not care. These guys love their girls back home. They aren't looking for a commitment and aren't interested in the details.

Dance, Colleen, say yes to any guy who asks you. Show some interest by putting a smile on your face and letting go of my arm. I love ya', girlfriend, but my feet are itchin' to hop to the beat. You'll be left standing alone in the dust unless you hop, too."

Colleen barely saw Liz again before midnight; the gentlemen wanted her attention. But Colleen was too preoccupied with her own suitors to notice. Liz was right. Once she looked a man in the eye and smiled, he was eager to take her hand. She danced all night until her feet hurt. It was a memorable party, second only to her wedding reception that was held beneath the tall oaks on the verdant, manicured lawn fringing the ornate St. Patrick's Church. Friends and family had encircled them, Tommy and Colleen. Everyone there cared about them.

Everyone here cared about each other. Tonight, these men and women ate, drank and acted as though there was a chance that someday soon, this war would end. They imagined standing in their own front yards, enveloped by those who longed for them. They pictured holding the newborn they had not yet seen. They prayed to pause at the grave of their deceased parent. They reflected on a horizon whose sun had not yet set on this whole bloody disaster.

SURVIVAL

Chapter Ten

A pint of sweat will save
a gallon of blood.

GENERAL GEORGE S. PATTON

❋ ❋ ❋

Under a simmering sun, Colleen stood and faced thirty-two student nurses on the hot tarmac. "You'll fly to battlefields on planes loaded with supplies and fresh troops," she reminded her charges on Monday. "You'll return on planes loaded with wounded. In between, anything can happen."

Nurses stood at attention, listening to her every word.

"Our job for the next five days is to practice our survival skills. We will hike and bivouac and make it on our own. We'll use camouflage to disguise ourselves, learn how to set up medical tents and how to secure food. There won't be a mess hall to feed us or a GE coffee pot. Our actions will control our fate. Be aware of your environment, avoid danger by thinking ahead. Now grab your packs and let's go."

The women tightened their helmets and adjusted their coveralls to march ten miles in formation with twenty-pound backpacks containing tents, sleeping mats and cooking gear. On the overgrown trail, the convoy moved slowly until they dropped their loads in a forest that was as impassable as the jungles in the South Pacific. Whacking the bush to clear space for the five pegs of their pup tents took all morning. The medical tents required a larger clearing. By nightfall, their shoulders ached and backs were stiff, but their shelters were sufficiently staked to withstand strong winds and tight enough to keep out the rain.

Dinner was a simple affair of beef jerky, plain hard biscuits from their mess kits and berries picked from the woods. They ate, then each one washed her dishes and rinsed them clean in hot water boiled in a pot hung over a roaring fire.

Resting now around the lingering flames, Mae Olson, whose good looks had only improved under the demands of grueling training, said, "I'm tired because of the physical labor, but I'm used to assisting Dr. Green six days a week in the office. He's the only kid doc in New London. We were open Monday through Saturday, so long hours aren't new to me."

Colleen joined the group, taking a seat in the circle next to Mae.

"I don't care how long the hours are. I'm getting paid for my work the same as the guys, thanks to the U. S. Army, so I'll give them their money's worth," said Emma Woodson. Her skills as a surgical nurse would prove very useful when treating a planeload of patients.

"Whatever we're paid, it's worth it. What we do are acts of hope," Iris Davis said. She had intuitively known how difficult taking orders would be for her and worked hard on self control. Her struggle with the military command structure strengthened her desire to assume that responsibility fully when it fell to her to do so. "We're standing up to Hirohito and Hitler, shoving our fingers in their faces. They'll never defeat us because we're stronger and smarter."

"You make it sound so easy," said Martha Eldon, whose empathy as a pediatric nurse applied to adult patients, too, "but they aren't going to give up. I've heard stories about those fiends that make me quiver. I bet even our generals quiver in their boots at the sight of them."

"England and France are under siege and counting on us to save them," said Emma. "I'm worried, too. We're in the fight of our lives, and we're not close to winning it."

"Hey, come on now, watch what you say," cautioned Mae. "We don't know the direction this war is going to take. We don't know what's true."

"Loose lips sink ships, isn't that what they tell us?" asked Mary Francis. She was the only one to experience air sickness, requiring several practice runs to acclimate to flight. Colleen had concerns about her stamina.

"Everything seems so random, not logical," said Catherine Duffy, who had become quite popular among the surgeons at Nichols, after they became aware of her skill set. One had relied on her expertise during an especially difficult emergency orthopedic procedure. "Look at the guys who came in on that plane Saturday. Whether a bullet finds you or not, it's random. It could be a nick on your knuckle, or your head blown off, it's random. Whether or not we get there in time, they have wounds we can treat, we can get them to a receiving hospital that's equipped for that soldier with that wound, all random. Those guys were ripped apart by shrapnel, bombs, machetes, fires, God knows what. In war, no one is immune, everyone is vulnerable and much of it doesn't make sense."

"Last week the field commander in Africa took one in the head. His rank offered him no protection from that bullet," said Lily Thompson. She found studying to be an air evacuation nurse a great relief after watching cancer patients die. Here, there was something she could do.

"The world is always in flux, it's always random and changing," said Iris.

"You're right, Iris," said Cora Schwartz, the only

Jewish woman in the group. "But this war will change how we see everything. It will wipe away our previous assumptions. We'll never be the same again after this, our country will never be the same. I don't know how things will be different, but this is a huge event in all our lives. It's going to leave a huge impression."

"Yes, even small variations can have big effects," said Iris, "and these are cataclysmic. We are being transformed for better or worse."

"I can't wait for everything to return to the way it was," said Catherine. "I was happy then, worked a good job, was saving for a house. Today all bets are off. If not for the Army, I might be unemployed and homeless."

"I wonder if there is a way to turn all this tumult into something useful. It is forcing us to rethink from the ground up how we do things. Maybe that will bring with it some advantages," said Colleen.

"Such as?" asked Emma, leaning forward to adjust the logs in the fire, causing sparks to pop and fly into the sky.

"Well, women have more opportunities, for one thing," she replied. "I've nursed since graduation and will continue to do so to support myself and my daughter. And I'm certain my sister, Sarah, who was a homemaker before the war, will not give up her new job at the county records office. She likes the people, likes the work, is skilled at reviewing the documents. It's more interesting than cleaning and laundry, and the money pays for groceries. She won't quit when this is over. If that's true for her, perhaps other women will also benefit by working outside the home."

"Maybe, but I agree with Emma. Only for equal pay. I'll never again work for less after knowing how good it feels to be valued the same as the men. I always thought I was just as good, of course, worth as much as them, but no one ever gave me the cash to prove they thought so, too," said Mary.

Everyone laughed in accord. Some toasted with their canteens.

"My salary pays for physical therapy," said Gretchen, whose determination helped her overcome the challenges the training demanded of her small stature. "My brother, Fritz, contracted polio three years ago, breathed through an iron lung for six months, was blessed to come out of it. He's so weak. He'll never walk after that, but he's trying therapy to regain use of his chest and arms, so he can take care of himself and breathe easier. My folks can't afford to pay for it. He's seventeen, my baby brother. For his sake, I'll stay with the Army as long as they'll keep me."

"The government paid for my education, I'm happy to pay my dues," said Jane Benton, school nurse.

"I'll join anything that exempts me from KP duty," said Cora. "I've got five brothers and have peeled enough potatoes to last my whole life. I wanted adventure as much as they did, so when they signed up, I did, too."

"I'll give the war credit for one thing," said Emma. "I've separated out those things that are meaningful from those that aren't."

"And what counts as meaningful are our flying togs," laughed Lily. "I can't wait to ditch my scrubs. Don't get me wrong, I'm proud of them, but those dress blues! With pants! They are so comfortable and easy to wear. I'm never taking them off."

"The leather jackets look so sharp," said Mae.

"Think of the effort we'll save washing, starching and ironing. I cleared $70 at the end of the month without having to spend on upkeep for my whites," said Catherine.

Everyone seemed drowsy, the evening wound down as the final embers glowed. It was a full minute before Catherine spoke again. "Why in the world are we sitting here in Louisville, Kentucky, in the woods, spied on by spiders, probably black widows? Their shiny, patent-leather bodies could sneak up on us any minute. Then they'll flash us with the red hourglasses on their backs and inject us with their poison. Here we sit, spiders poised to poison us, mosquitoes enjoying our flesh and blood for their dessert, while we eat leather for supper. Why are we here?"

"We're in Louisville because of the '37 flood," said Colleen. "When high water demolished this city, Bowman Field's high elevation meant clear runways for planes flying in food. Every place else was buried under debris---roads washed out, railway timbers floating in ditches, bridges hanging by twisted steel threads. Bowman's strategic advantage became obvious."

"Maybe so, but I'd rather be in the Appalachian Mountains," said Mary. "I've hiked the trail from Georgia to West Virginia. I'm going to finish up in Maine when this thing is over."

"I like the hospitality here. What's wrong with being in a river city that appreciates music, fabulous food and fine horses?" asked Gretchen. "My boyfriend took me to the Derby last May and bought me the cutest little red hat. The infield at the racetrack is wild with people, but we sat in the grandstand. Drinking a julep and seeing those magnificent animals, what a great day that was. Ed looked so adorable in his seersucker suit and straw boater."

"That's what I miss most, those special moments I used to take for granted," said Mary. "My best friend, Julie, meeting me for lunch at the Woolworth's counter. We'd talk too long and be late for our next appointment. Or seeing my sweet Grandpa waiting for me in his rocking chair on the front porch. Granny would bring out a tray of cookies, and we would talk all afternoon about nothing. It was sublime, no blood, no one sick, just weather reports and how the tomatoes were growing. It's been months since I've seen them. Who knows when I'll return to that swing?"

"How on earth did we get ourselves into this predicament?" asked Emma. "I mean, I know the

Japs blew up Pearl Harbor, but how did the world become such a mess?"

"We didn't do anything to cause this mess. You and I and the rest of us are nobodies," said Catherine. "This is a deadly game being played by madmen on the world stage."

"You may be nobodies, but you're damn good nurses," Colleen said, wearing a thoughtful look. "We're at our best when someone is in trouble. Because of that, we will help midwife order out of the muddle we're in. We will help with the healing."

"When Sandberg Elementary closes for the summer," said Jane, "I paint in oils. My favorite pieces evolved from muddle. My canvas starts out badly, but I keep adding paint until something pleasing manifests. Maybe life after the armistice will be like that."

"Only if we win," said Gretchen. "Just imagine if Hitler does."

"He's a painter. Watercolors," said Jane.

"Apparently not a successful one, if he has time to fight a war," said Emma.

"Maybe if he had succeeded, he would have had no interest in starting a war," said Jane.

"Are you saying if we rush out to buy Hitler's watercolors, compare him to Max Ernst and fawn over him with fame, he'll be persuaded to call this whole thing off?" asked Emma.

"Yes," said Jane. "At an earlier time, if his ego had been assuaged with acclaim as an artist, that might have been enough for him. He wouldn't have wanted more."

"People like Hitler always want more," said Mae. "Nothing will satiate him until he rules the world. This ugly, horrid war is because of his lust for power."

"And the sneaky Japanese, they also lust for power," Gretchen said. "Who knows what they're up to?"

"I never thought of Japan until Pearl Harbor," said Emma. "After this, I will never think of it in the same way."

"So many more people will be hurt or killed. Why don't the citizens of the world just call off the war?" asked Jane. "Refuse to fight. Politicians got us into this. Why don't we, the citizens of the world, the ones actually stuck in this muck, why don't we rise up and say 'no, stop this insanity, we're going home'?"

"You're very naive. Have you ever seen a German soldier? Do you think they are going to quit?" asked Martha.

"If we don't want to fight, maybe their soldiers don't want to, either. We could appeal to their better natures and demand that the world's leaders join to declare a state of peace instead of war."

"Have you heard Hitler speak?" asked Mae. "Right ain't in him. Power is his aphrodisiac. He controls the message, the military and the money. His people follow him. He's not gonna' say goodbye to all that and wave a white flag, and the German people aren't gonna' make him."

"Armistice for World War I," said Martha, "the war to end all wars, was on November 11, 1918. On December 7, 1941, we entered World War II. When this one is finished, there will be another one. The history of civilization is the history of warfare. War is about power---who has it and will kill to keep it, who doesn't have it but will kill to get it."

"This whole thing is a lot more complicated than just one fanatical fuhrer or maniacal emperor," said Gretchen.

"Yes, it's about innocent victims, brute force, politics, personal charisma and fame and fortune for a few," said Mae. "Those who somehow manage to profit, to make big money off the bloodshed."

"Yeah," said Martha, "while the rest of us wonder if we're going to have anything left."

"Peace is not out of the question, but I agree there are many in power with vested interests in keeping the chaos going. To get our men home, we'll have to put those guys out of business first," said Emma.

"Well, in my humble opinion, macho does not prove mucho," said Catherine. "Hitler's all bluff, a blowhard who's probably startled by his shadow. He has the brain of an amoeba and is nothing but a mean bully, a small man using his huge power to destroy us all. He hides behind all that rhetoric and the Nazi salutes, but it's the young men he conscripts, who sign up out of patriotic duty, who do the killing, and dying, for him, the coward. I bet he doesn't have the balls of a mouse."

"Let's pray Roosevelt's balls, and Churchill's, are bigger," said Martha.

"Why does it always have to be about whose balls are biggest? We deserve something better than that, don't' we? I happen to think something better is poised to emerge, once we get to the other side of this," said Jane.

"You, dear one, are trying to satisfy your desire to find paradise lost," said Martha. "You will be disappointed; your dreams will not come true."

"I'm a realist," said Jane, "not a dreamer. If enough of us are convinced peace should happen, it will. We'll reach a consensus of opinion, a tipping point. We'll demand an end to fighting. We'll devote our aid and resources to activities that make peace. That make the world a better place for everyone to live. Only then will we have it."

"That sounds foolish. How could it ever happen?" asked Martha.

Jane leaned forward and held her sweaty bandana over what was left of the flames in a futile attempt to dry it. "We have to let this notion roll over us like a tidal wave," she said. "Let it gain strength until it transforms our thinking. Picture the water flowing through the Grand Canyon. A trickle becomes a roaring river that polishes pebbles into gems. Powerful ideas flow just like that."

This image invoked optimism. Could it be true?

Colleen felt overwhelmed as she paused and considered. She shifted her position to regain control and noticed that others were open to the suggestion, too, pondering the prospects for a ceasefire and cordial tranquility.

"I agree that real power exists in the human heart, and we reach it through our personal connections, which have been so broken by all this turmoil," Cora said. "My Jewish grandparents immigrated from Warsaw. Do any of you have German blood?"

Gretchen raised her hand.

"They say Hitler cleaned out the ghetto by rounding up Jews for slaughter," said Cora. "Yet here we are together, serving on the same side, both paying a price. We've learned tolerance for each other."

"War hurts everyone," agreed Iris. "It makes savages of us all. But the President says we have to fight the Nazis and avenge Pearl Harbor."

"I get that," said Jane. "I also get that when we learn we'll sink or swim together, we'll find a way to swim our way out of this. Maybe it is wishful thinking, but I believe it."

"Until that happens, how do we keep Hitler's army from marching down Fifth Avenue into Saks?" asked Mae.

"You know what will bring this to an end? Total annihilation, us or them. Who would you rather it be?" asked Martha.

"I'm fine with total annihilation, as long as it's them," said Mae.

"Then what?" asked Jane.

"Then we're done," said Mae.

"Then we'll reconnect with all we've missed," Cora said, "return to all that we depend on."

"We could be one second away from total destruction, or a second away from a total turnaround of this intolerable situation, depending on what we choose," said Jane. "Eventually that will become clear to us."

"I feel like we're going to have to construct a whole new world when this is over," said Iris.

"Where will we begin?" Mary asked.

"Have you ever seen Notre Dame?" said Jane. "It began with a single brick."

GRADUATION

Chapter Eleven

Age wrinkles the body. Quitting wrinkles the soul.

GENERAL DOUGLAS MACARTHUR

❋ ❋ ❋

The final two days of bivouac started out clear and sunny, which made it somewhat easier for the nurses to complete the same infiltration course that gives soldiers a taste of battle. From a holding station on the banks of the Ohio River, low branches snapped in their faces as they walked single file. Briars grabbed their ankles and scratched their legs. Snakes slithered alongside as natural companions.

For the next forty-eight hours, each pair of

nurses would survive on their wits or fail the program. If they could not read their compass, they would become lost in the dense woods. If they could not scavenge for food, they would be hungry. If they could not manage confrontations with wildlife and faux landmine blasts, they would not walk across the stage to graduate. If they could not crawl over rough terrain, under barbed wire fences, through all kinds of muck, if they could not handle blank mortars whizzing by a few inches above their heads and ammunition shot by "enemy" firing fake machine guns, they would not receive the gold wings of a Second Lieutenant flight nurse. In this final test on a vivid, simulated battlefront, if they could not apply emergency first aid, identify and treat infections, bandage wounds, stop hemorrhages, apply CPR to restart a heart after sudden cardiac arrest, administer oxygen and intravenous meds, check dog tags for blood type and perform transfusions, splint broken bones and minister to men in shock, the dream these women shared to serve the USA Army Air Corps as air evacuation nurses would not come true.

When Captain Chantel designated Colleen for this role, she had admonished, "Your job is to help these nurses find the best in themselves." Colleen looked over the class, standing in formation, waiting for her direction. She deemed the mission complete, satisfied with all their accomplishments, and hers, too. These exceptional professionals had mastered the art of nursing and modelled excellence in unique and challenging circumstances. Every one of these remarkable, resilient women had proven her strength was sufficient to command a flying medical ward.

Graduation was held the next day. Family members could not travel to attend, except for those who lived nearby. Two sisters and one mother formed the audience along with a smattering of officers and staff.

In the chapel near the women's barracks, the band sat on a platform colorfully decorated with flags and tall, green palms. It played a lively "God Bless America" as nurses lined up in formation. They each wore their full-dress uniforms---regulation grey slacks, white shirts, black ties, stylish blue jackets designed similar to those worn by the Brits, gray gloves and black oxfords. They had measured for their ensembles the day before, after their showers removed a week's worth of grime and the battlefield mud bath. Clean hair and new clothes, head to toe, excited them. They reveled in both. They were ready.

The music ceased prior to the invocation given by Captain Wood, a flying ace of World War I. Then Brigadier General Paul Borman, the Air Surgeon, climbed the steps to the stage and cleared his throat to speak.

"Graduating today are thirty-two air

evacuation nurses who face quick action," he began. "You will receive an immediate call to duty in combat zones in unknown parts of the world. Your commitment is no less than that of every other member of our armed forces, a willingness to risk your lives for your country in service to others. The responsibility for patients in your care falls on you, until the destination is reached. After six weeks of rigorous achievement, you graduate today as Second Lieutenants. We're mighty glad to have you join us and welcome you to our ranks. Congratulations and good luck."

The women knew all this already, no explanation was necessary, but it was nice to hear an officer in his position affirm their status publicly, firmly, proudly. *Why did having the approval of a man make their accomplishments seem more worthwhile?* It didn't. *Why wasn't their own approval enough?* It was.

No matter. The smiling nurses with jaunty caps perched on their heads filed past one by one to receive their flight nurse's wings and diplomas, then returned to their seats. The carefully printed documents in their hands represented faith in themselves, the perseverance to overcome obstacles and a commitment to manage changes and surmount difficulties in every sliver of life. It offered the prospect of encountering adventure head on, whatever it may bring, and meeting the longing of their nurturing nature.

They applauded, along with the dignitaries,

when the Brigadier General awarded Mae Olson a medal for earning the highest grade in class. A flock of cameramen swooped in to record the notable event in newsreels.

After dismissal, nurses demonstrated their routine practices assisting the wounded for the benefit of the newspapermen, who wanted photographs for the front page of the Courier-Journal, the Chicago Tribune and the Cincinnati Enquirer. When they asked to interview the instructor, Nurse O'Brien, she deferred saying, "These women are heroic. If you really want to know what it's like, ask them."

Tomorrow, these accomplished nurses would don their new flight uniforms, lift their packs onto their backs and climb aboard C-47s to fly to their fate.

CLARITY

Chapter Twelve

Pessimism never won any battle.

GENERAL DWIGHT D. EISENHOWER

❋ ❋ ❋

"**M**ama, thank you for the picture of Chloe holding Daisy. Sweet kitty! She looks so peaceful in Chloe's lap, and "C" is elated. It means the world to me to see her face. She has grown so much! Her hair is so long! I like it parted on the side with the bow. Thank you for taking such good care of my precious girl."

Colleen held the pencil to her temple as if the words would magically pass from her brain to the paper, but no muse hid there. As she struggled to compose her thoughts, Liz popped around the corner. "Whatcha' doing, sailor?"

Liz could always make her smile. "Not much, trying to write a letter. You?"

"I'm getting the gang together to go to the matinee at the Vogue. Want to go?"

"What's showing?"

"*For Whom the Bell Tolls* with Gary Cooper. Come with us."

"I really should stay here and finish this, but I sure would like to see it."

"That can wait until we get back. I need a day of rest to recover from our hiking trip at Mammoth Cave yesterday. You need one, too. Did you have fun?"

"I did. The caverns look amazing inside."

"Don't they? I'm glad we got to see them. Those USO gals knock themselves out trying to make our lives here more pleasant, give 'em credit for that. You also gotta give yourself a break occasionally if you want to stay sharp. Otherwise, your brain becomes a noodle and you won't have anything left for the guys who need you. So come on, let's have a bit more fun before we report to duty tomorrow."

"When does the movie begin?"

"That's my girl! It starts at 1400. Be at the door at 1300."

"That gives me enough time to get this done, so I'll meet you then---looking forward to it as much as you are." And she was. Liz had become a confidante and trusted friend. They connected. Liz was interesting and cared about everyone, including her. Colleen always learned something useful from Liz and liked how she found the irony in any situation. She could make Colleen laugh at herself. Liz often offered a funny, but wise, perspective on whatever subject they discussed. Colleen craved that kind of clarity; Liz gave it.

When Colleen met up with Liz, she stood alone. "Where is everyone?"

"Turns out Harriet has cramps and is hunched over a water bottle. Rita is lunching at a barbecue cookout with a local family today, lucky her. Millie saw the movie last week with her boyfriend. So, it's just you and me, kid."

"Hope Rita brings us leftovers," Colleen said as she opened the door.

"She promised she would. I drool thinking about them. Anyway, Corporal Buckley is our chauffeur. He's giving us a ride, he said, 'cause it's the least he could do after the good nurses at Nichols patched his arm back together."

They climbed out of the Corporal's jeep onto the busy Lexington Avenue corner and did their best to avoid traffic while crossing the street. Next door to the theater stood a small, quaint cafe known for good food, The Parsley House. "Hey, I've got a good idea," Liz said, as she often did.

"And what might that be?"

"We're early, it's forty-five minutes before the show starts. Why don't we duck in here for a bite?"

"It would be nice to eat something that doesn't taste like potatoes."

"Then let's go in," said Liz, pointing the way.

The waitress recited the menu and convinced them the chicken soup was the perfect dish to have, along with a slice of sour dough bread and a piece of chess pie. Soon, she set silverware, iced tea and hot bowls on the table.

"I saw you were writing home this morning. What have you heard from your folks? Everything ok with Chloe?" Liz asked, between breaths to cool her soup.

Colleen tore the bread into two servings and handed one to Liz before spreading butter on the second and placing it on her plate. "She's doing great, but Tommy's been fired. He lost his Class II occupational draft deferment. His job as foreman at the factory had exempted him from service. He was more valuable to Uncle Sam's war effort making rope for the navy's ships than he was serving on one. I don't know what happens to him now."

"Why was he fired?"

"Mama says he got in a fist fight with one of his men, whose father happens to be their number one advocate in the government supply office. The father demanded Tommy be fired and, it turns out, his boss was happy to oblige. Tommy's temper has caused him problems before."

"Whoa! All that fighting! What is fueling his anger? What's gnawing on him?"

"I don't know," Colleen said, stirring the sugar into her tea.

"Your husband knocks you out, he punches a guy he supervises. Something must be churning inside. He is still your husband, isn't he? You're not divorced yet?"

"No, my divorce isn't final. Tommy won't give me permission. He's blocking me every step of the way."

"Thank heavens your parents are protecting Chloe. Do you think he would hurt her?"

"I really don't know. I didn't think he would hurt me. But Mama is a photographer and took pictures of the bruises on my face. She told Tommy to stay away, or she'd get him arrested and charged."

"What can you do to speed up the divorce?"

"Mama and Papa are looking for someone to help me find a way out, but Tommy wants to make it as hard as possible. Mama says there's lots of things he can do to keep me tied up and trapped. He's using Chloe as leverage to get what he wants, because he knows I'll give it to him. Maybe I should call him. I haven't talked to him in six months. Maybe I could reason with him." She put her spoon back in the bowl and stared out the window.

"He doesn't sound very reasonable," Liz said, snapping her back to reality. "He sounds as if he gets his kicks beating people up."

Colleen lifted her spoon again. By now the broth was cool in her mouth. "I can't be too hard on him. I still care about Tommy. Apparently, he broke a tooth in the fight and looks dreadful." She looked away and her eyes filled with tears.

"Look at me, Colleen. Listen. Detach yourself from his problems. They aren't yours, and you can't solve them. He has to."

"He'll be lost without his buddies at the factory. Tommy's always been a hard worker, spent a lot of hours on the job. Of course, he thought that entitled him to drink a couple of beers with the guys at Flanagan's at the end of every shift. I'd feed Chloe, put her to bed and wait to eat dinner with him, often at nine or ten o'clock by the time he came home. I had an early schedule and never got enough sleep. Boy-oh-boy, did I pay an on-the-job penalty for that! I worried I'd make a mistake some days, hurt a patient, make a poor assessment because I was so tired."

"And still he persisted?" asked Liz, wiping her napkin against her lips. She had the most beautiful curve to her mouth, which looked luscious even with the lipstick rubbed off.

"I talked to Tommy about it, told him I needed to get to bed earlier, or I might screw up and hurt someone, but he never stopped going to the bar. Drinking with his pals mattered more than having dinner with us, more than cuddling with me. He'd drink too much, then stumble to bed expecting sex, but the smell of alcohol on his breath was such a turn off. I had a hard time doing it, even when I wanted to."

"Yeah, that does sound pretty disgusting."

"But now he's lost me, and his status as head

honcho at the plant, and his excuse to hang out with his buddies at the bar. What will become of him?" She shook her head and stared at the table in despair.

"Was he a drinker when you said, 'I do'? Had he hit you before?"

"I knew he liked a cold beer, so did his daddy, but he had never hit me. I do remember once, when we were in fifth grade, I found him playing in the side yard, which was unusual. Our mothers insisted we play in the back yards, so they could watch us from their kitchen windows. It was news to me when I realized we could be hidden from their view for a few minutes by moving around the corner.

"I followed him there and found Tommy huddled over a dead cat. I asked what happened, he said the cat had accidentally drowned in a puddle from the rainstorm the night before. That didn't make a lot of sense, I'd never known a cat to drown in a puddle, but I didn't question him. I trusted Tommy."

"An unlikely story."

"Oh, there's more. The cat's throat was slit; Tommy was holding the knife. When I asked what he was doing, he said he was conducting an autopsy. That seemed a fishy explanation, too, but I just let it go. I thought he didn't want me to tell on him and get him in trouble, but he knew I would never do that."

Liz cut the dessert and divided the pieces

between the two of them. She placed a bite on her tongue. The flavor was sweet and delicious. "Sounds like someone who hides things and finds it difficult to tell the truth, Colleen. Sounds like someone showing you who he really is. When will you believe him?"

"The way he acted did make me think he was up to something. I just didn't know what. We did a thousand things together growing up, but that is the one thing I never forgot. Does a boy slitting a cat's throat make a man a monster?"

"I don't know, but there could be a bigger picture that you don't see. We know husbands can be deadly. In the emergency room, I've seen too many wives lose their lives."

"After I married Tommy, I saw his dad smack his mother around one Thanksgiving. It scared me because I really was not aware he did that. It scared me more that no one acted as if Mr. O'Brien's behavior was wrong. When I told Mama, she seemed concerned but not surprised."

"She probably already knew it, but I'm guessing she didn't know the son had learned to abuse at his father's knee."

"After one of their fights, Tommy walked out of his parents' house and kicked his dog, Rufus. Gave him a swift, hard boot to the side. He didn't know I was behind him. He shouldn't have done it and said he was sorry. I don't think he meant to hurt Rufus. He'd just had it, you know? Just couldn't take it anymore. He was tired of listening to another one of their shouting matches."

"Yet, he hit you when it suited him. You still have unfinished business with him, Colleen, that isn't going away until you deal with it. Tommy abused you. Accept the truth of what is, then go from there. Seems to me being here is a huge first step. When you return to Ithaca and Chloe, you can close that circle."

"I never saw any of this coming. That's what shocks me the most. When it happened on New Year's Day, I cried, I yelled, but I forgave him. He made a mistake and said so. When he blackened my eye in February, I grabbed Chloe and left. I should have known."

"Women rarely do. You're too hard on yourself, Colleen. Stop the blaming. It's not helpful and only brings you down. Use your strength on productive things that build up your can-do spirit, 'cause you're gonna need it."

"I sure am. I'm twenty-two-years old, and my love life is over."

"Your life didn't end when you fell to the floor, Colleen, it began. Ridding yourself of your abuser is a victory. Now that he's gone, there are things you can do to get through this, but first know what it is you want. Don't be coy, say what you mean, mean what you say."

"I don't know if I can. Tommy was always in charge of making decisions."

"And he decided to hit you. Twice. He could have killed you, Colleen. He might still if you give him another chance. I get that this new reality has upended your perfect little world, but it wasn't very perfect, was it? And losing it doesn't mean you are worse off. You saved yourself. You saved your daughter. Congratulations. You're earning money, succeeding at your job and making your way. You can make decisions; you decide for patients every day. Decide for yourself, too."

"I don't know where to begin." Colleen twisted her napkin nervously around her fingers.

"Think through the outcome you want and what you'll do to get there. It's not necessary to know all the answers right now, but it is important to take the next steps, whatever they may be. Bringing order out of chaos is what we do. I know we're crazy busy running through each day, and our lives are structured around our strict routines. But all this structure and busyness brings stability in the middle of a huge, tangled mess. That enables you and me to tend to ourselves and everybody else. We're in a good place. An attitude of gratitude will help you see that."

"Oh, I know we are." She looked at Liz with a faint but certain smile, recognizing how lucky she was to be there, at that table, across from Liz.

"At the hospital, in the classroom, the parts of your life that you manage, not Tommy, you know what to do and assume responsibility for your actions. What else can I say, beyond that, which will convince you that you can do this, too? And that the U. S Army Air Corps has your back?

Channel your negative worry into something positive. Stay strong, stay true, stand up for yourself," she said, patting the top of Colleen's hands resting on the table.

"What would I do without you, Liz?" she asked. Her gaze was direct and focused on her friend. "I might not have made it through this if you hadn't been here to keep me going. Please know how much I appreciate you."

She knew Liz's concern was sincere and her counsel thoughtful, but her best gift of kinship was how well she could see all sides of a situation and outline the destructive patterns, like those in Colleen's relationship with Tommy. Through Liz, she could recognize the folly in her reasoning. Liz's pithy comments gave her more food for thought than all of Father O'Malley's sermons combined.

"Then do me a favor, Colleen," Liz countered. "Remember that Tommy doesn't control you unless you let him. Claim your power. That's the only way you'll get it. He's not going to give it to you."

"I don't feel like I have any power."

"Bless your heart," Liz laughed. "You take charge of every situation you're in."

"You do, too, Liz, you're a take-charge girl if ever there was one. Look what you're doing to find Van. What about him, have you heard anything more?"

The waitress removed their dishes and handed them the bill. They counted out their dollars and waited for change. After she left, Liz said, "All my leads are dead ends. I write everyone I can think of who might help. I get return envelopes that have been opened, containing form letters that have been read, that reveal no useful information. Not one person has been helpful so far. I must get on one of those planes headed for the Pacific and go find out for myself what happened to him, or I will lose my mind."

"Well, what's stopping you? I've got fresh recruits starting Monday. You could be one of them."

"No, I couldn't. I flunked the entrance exam. There are twenty applicants for every opening, and I can't pass the darn test. I know I can do whatever they need, but they'll never let me in to prove it to them."

Colleen leaned forward with interest. "Liz, you're an excellent nurse. If anyone can complete the course, you can. What's the problem with the test?"

"It's not this test, it's any test. I've always been like that. I learn from doing, not reading, and can never show what I know with pencil and paper. They want a piece of written proof they can stick in a file."

"I don't get it. You're a more experienced nurse than I am. Why can't you pass?"

"I wish I knew. Ever since I started school I panic, because I've received so many bad scores. Do you have any idea how humiliating it is to fail over and over, when you think you know it? Something's wrong with my noggin. Words get garbled when I try to read them. I just can't study and take a test, and teachers always insist that I do."

"Liz, maybe I can help you." Coleen felt the excitement of one who knows how to proceed.

"You can't help me, no one can. I nearly flunked out of Missouri State, couldn't pass the tests there, either. I studied so hard; it didn't do any good. I only got through by the hair on my chinny chin chin because the dean of the school liked me and got me tutors all the way through. Her help and influence with the faculty, plus the excellent reviews I received on my clinicals, convinced them to cut me just enough slack to slide under the bar."

"If you want to be a flight nurse, Liz, I can get you through the course. Let's go see Captain Dorsey tomorrow, first thing. We'll get you enrolled. If this is really what you want, we can make it happen."

"You think so? You think I could be an air evac nurse? That is my dream come true. I am so impatient to find Van. I really want to fly on one of those planes and go see where he's been."

"I know you can do it. You'll be a stellar student." Colleen's confidence was genuine.

"Did I ever tell you how we met?"

"No, you didn't."

"I was late for my shift one day and took a streetcar to get to work. Usually, I walked the eight blocks. Van had broken his ankle snow skiing and rode the same car, sat in the seat opposite me. He started a conversation, and four months later, we married in front of the Justice of the Peace, just before he flew out. It was quick and small with just Ma and my sisters there. Poor Ma, she was nearly apoplectic, doesn't like surprises at all. That one was a doozy."

"You must have good karma to find him when you did."

"The smallest coincidence can change your entire life, can't it?"

"We'll change yours tomorrow, Liz. I promise you we will."

They left a tip on the table for the waitress and entered the theater under the marquee with Gary Cooper's name flashing in white lights. The usher tore their tickets and tossed them into a box. Colleen settled in a quiet corner, Liz joined her soon with a striped box of butterless popcorn to share and two red-and-white paper cups of Coca-Cola fizzing over ice.

As the movie neared the end, the shrill siren of the Civil Defense Corps blew so loudly that the film stopped. Another blackout tonight, an auspice. When they left the theater and ventured outside, a gully washer downpour had soaked an earth that was going dark as each light was extinguished. They flagged a taxi, and as they rode home, the sky's iridescence reflected through the inky black, as if to strengthen the willpower of these two souls, evolving beyond the points on their compasses.

FLYBOY

Chapter Thirteen

*History does not long entrust the care
of freedom to the weak or the timid.*

GENERAL DWIGHT D. EISENHOWER

✻ ✻ ✻

It was 2100 when the distress signal blared.
Instantly, everyone knew the moment they'd
prepared for had come and returned to the
hospital at once. In the morning announcements,
Captain Chantel had said base hospitals all over
the country were overloaded from the surge in the
number of wounded and couldn't handle more.
Nichols and other inland hospitals would step up
and receive a greater share of these warriors. A
full load would arrive sometime today. The staff
did not know their names, where they're from
or where they fell. They only knew something
terrible had happened to them.

Air evac nurse Second Lieutenant Jane Benton,

a member of Colleen's first Bowman graduating class, tended patients during the flight. With practiced precision, she directed the medics to unload the men from the plane and wheel them to the ambulance for the ride down the runways to Nichols. Once there, staff nurses and doctors met them at the door and took charge, relying on her recommendations to triage patients.

Grimy men in torn and filthy clothes, missing shoes, glasses and helmets, but with a cigarette still tucked behind an ear, lay moaning, uncovered, on stretchers in every available space. Their faces wore pale, drawn expressions with glassy eyes. They groaned in pain from their tattered bodies, gaping wounds, missing limbs, broken bones, swollen feet, discolored skin. The medical staff huddled over each one, planning the course of action.

"Nurse Kizer," Dr. Carlson Babcock shouted over the din, "take this one into an empty room and get started. It appears he has all burns, nothing broken, but they're extensive. He's in a lot of trouble, but if I don't operate now, PFC Kenneth Blakesly will bleed to death within the hour. Can you handle this?"

"Yes, Doctor, I've given saline baths before. Temperature at 105 degrees?"

"Yes, that's the best we can do. Let's prep him for grafts. Call a plastic surgeon. Ask for Sloan. See if you can find some Bunyan bags to wrap him. And Liz, keep your eye on his vitals. If they start to go, start resuscitation and send someone to find me. I don't care where I am, got it?"

"Got it."

Liz and an orderly wheeled the man into a room and lifted him onto the bed. With a glance, she could see the patient's injuries were grave, his anguish intense. This torture would be long-lasting.

She unrolled the gauze bandage that completely covered his face and fell backwards, almost tripping over the ventilator pushing air into his lungs. His horrendous burns had melted the entire left side and contorted him into a monstrous expression. A burned-out socket was missing an eyeball and a hole was open where half his nose should have been. His scalp was raw, and the veins pulsated wildly through what was left of a thin, crisp layer of blackened skin, wet with tiny puddles of bodily fluids weeping in the folds.

Yet something about him seemed familiar. She had seen him somewhere. Then it hit her. His ring was the clue. This was Jeff Winters, the fly boy who wanted to return to Texas and marry his hometown girl, Jenny. Whenever he said her name, he had twisted the carved wooden band around his left third finger, the one that Jen had placed there until they could marry and exchange it for the real thing. Will had teased him about it, called it a ring through the nose. But Jeff was undaunted and didn't mind the ribbing of his brothers. All in a night's fun.

With burns like these, Jeff may not live to see Jen again. He may not see tomorrow.

His injuries were so severe, Liz knew she must move quickly. She needed assistance and ran to the door to call for help. Nurses leaned over every patient, tending to them. Doctors ran from one injured soldier to the next. *I am on my own,* she thought.

"Get Nurse O'Brien," she yelled at the desk clerk. "She should be in the barracks. Tell her it's all-hands-on-deck. I need her ASAP. Hurry!"

Colleen entered the room gowned, masked, ready. "What's the emergency, Liz?" she asked.

"It's Jeff Winters. He's got first and second degree burns on his arms and legs, third degree on his face. We gotta fix him fast. Get the fluids started."

Colleen walked toward the patient and lost the air in her lungs as she gasped in shock. Jeff, that strong, virile man was reduced to a barely conscious human, crying in agony and running out of time.

Her instincts kicked in. She hung the drip and held his right hand where flesh remained intact, stroking him gently. "The debriding will be excruciating," she whispered to Liz. "Can you give him more morphine?"

"He's received the maximum dose. It didn't knock him out. I don't know how he's still awake. It's critical that we thoroughly soak him in saline, remove the burned skin and apply the ointment. We'll wrap his arms and legs in Bunyans. The surgeon is on his way and will start the reconstruction on his face. Let's keep going until he calls for Jeff. Can you find the burn bags? They have the antiseptics, tools and bandages in them."

"He's writhing with pain. How can we hold him still?" Colleen asked, searching cabinets for the supplies.

"We'll each do a small section. I've started on his head. You take a look at his feet. Don't dawdle, his vitals are weak."

Liz and Colleen stayed focused through the night, using saline baths to soften the dead skin, delicately positioning tools to remove it piece by piece in thin strips and small bits, gently rubbing his raw flesh with salve, wrapping his useless limbs in the oil-silk Bunyan envelopes and his face in white sterile gauze to allow healing air in.

It took a toll. It's dreadfully difficult to witness the real distress of hundreds of men and remain placid, and Colleen had known shellshock before. This one was different. This was Jeff, the great guy with huge passions and unflinching love. Nothing should go wrong for a man like him. He's too good. Yet here he was, at this moment, aching over every movement of his body, every touch, begging for a breath, wondering what is left for him, if he is capable of thought, wanting his Jen to remember him like he was, never like this.

Somehow, Colleen would have to make it

through the next weeks knowing Jeff would be forced to tolerate unfathomable suffering through the next years. Concentration would be difficult. The war drags on, no end in sight. Yearning for peace had set in long ago. Every day was an effort to avoid depression and discouragement. This day was the worst yet.

DUTY

Chapter Fourteen

*In preparing for battle, I have
always found that plans are useless,
but planning is indispensable.*

GENERAL DWIGHT D. EISENHOWER

✳ ✳ ✳

The twenty-four most recent Army Air Corps Evacuation School graduates, poised to join a squadron on a minute's notice, awaited their assignments. Colleen found Liz cramming her flight bag full of gear. She picked up the gas mask from the foot of the bed and handed it to her friend. "Don't forget your new fashion accessory," she said.

Liz hung it from her arm and made room in the bag to stuff it in. Her footlocker was already crammed with everything she could take when she is sent overseas.

She still couldn't believe she'd received her wings. Colleen had managed to get her through the class by being the first person to accept that she did not learn like others do, who didn't tell her to "just try harder," as every other teacher had insisted. Instead, Colleen listened to Liz's take on the situation, joked with her about her unique style and convinced her to learn in spite of it. Colleen noted that Liz transposed "b"s and "d"s when she wrote. Liz noted she did not comprehend what she read.

Colleen turned out to be a teacher who thrived on challenge. She observed that Liz, an exceptional nurse with astute instincts, who practiced the true art of nursing every day, stumbled over written descriptions of tasks she completed on a regular basis. Seeing that, Colleen began showing Liz how to use other clues to decipher meaning--- the charts and graphs, pictures and headings, definitions of keywords, summary sentences--- simple techniques that broke difficult concepts into edible bites.

Liz and Maureen Doogan, another nurse who asked for help, met with Colleen nightly after class. Together, the three of them plowed through the material until both were certain to pass the exam. They did. Now they eagerly accepted their posts aboard a hospital plane.

"Where are you going?" Colleen asked.

"Don't know," said Liz. "Colonel Jenkins said report at 0600. We'll find out then."

"Anything I can do to help?"

"Nah, I've got it. I do ask a favor, though."

"Sure, anything. What's up?"

Liz pulled a folder from a box below her bunk and handed it to Colleen. "My final papers, my will and such. Please hold on to them for me, will you? If something happens, you can mail them to my Ma. The address is in there."

"Oh, Liz, nothing's going to get in your way."

"I plan to duck all cannonballs, but just in case, Ma will receive my insurance. It would really help relieve her gloom about me leaving. She thinks I'm abandoning her and the family."

"I'll hang on to these for you and give them back when you return, you hear me?"

"I hear ya', darlin'. I will do all I can to keep my head on my shoulders, and two feet planted firmly on the ground, not under it," Liz said, throwing her slender arms around Colleen's neck, holding her close. Their embrace held warmth and kindness and gratitude in it; a viable, sturdy, important force between them. A treasure.

"Thank you, dear friend, for getting me through the class and on the next plane out. I couldn't have done it without you."

"My pleasure, Liz. You are going to serve your country and do a great job saving lives. They're lucky to have you. And when this is over, when you return to us, Van will walk beside you. That's the vision we'll hold on to, until you can make it so."

It took two weeks before Colleen learned that Liz had shipped out on a transport plane that ran routes somewhere in the Pacific. She got the map out to locate the region. Liz was in the area of the Solomon Islands, not exactly where Van was last known to be, Guadalcanal, but in the right island chain in the right ocean. She was getting closer. Liz was certain some of the guys there would know of him, as she wrote in a letter to Colleen, describing what she'd seen. The envelope had been slit, as overseas mail often was, and no contraband fell out. Colleen eagerly pulled out four pages and started reading the dainty script.

August 1943

Hi, Colleen,

This is the first hour I've had to myself since last I saw you at our beloved Bowman and went on duty in the field of the wild blue yonder. When I left on the sixteenth, we flew thirty straight hours to Horaniu, where the Japs drop bombs on our sailors like tossing candy in a parade. You can't imagine the terror of not knowing when the next one will hit, or where. Then we moved to Henderson Field, our airbase in the Eastern Solomons, where we live in daily fear of the enemy and their ammunition coming our way.

The action has not stopped. If I'm not flying, I'm bent over a table in the field hospital. We're so busy, my bladder almost explodes before I get to a bathroom, an outdoor shack in the back. I'm tired when I go to bed, but the noise is so disturbing, I can't stay asleep, even though my next shift is eight, or fewer, hours away. I've lost about fifteen pounds, guessing by the way my slacks slide down my hips because of the less than delicious food, constant work and dripping sweat.

The jungle's so thick you can't see two feet in front, gunfire is all around and mosquitos as big as birds attack my face. Reptiles, including crocodiles, own the place. As you may recall, I did not appreciate our bivouac week, or anything that slithered, but I'm sure glad you put me through it. Nothing could have properly primed me for this, but at least I have a notion of what to do, and how to survive, in this wilderness. All the rest has to be figured out as I go.

The natives haven't had many encounters with white women who look like us, so they stare, when they get a chance. One even wanted to touch my arm to sample my skin.

The officers initially were wary of us, but the enlisted men are elated we are here. It's been a while since our guys have seen an American woman. They respond with great enthusiasm, shall we say, when we show up, waving and screaming loud enough to embarrass us. They are every age, rank and personality type, all pining for their women.

Some of the men, younger than me mentally or chronologically, are impulsive and become easily infatuated, making serving with them awkward. I've rejected three proposals from married guys missing their wives and seeking comfort in a quickie romance.

Our living quarters are primitive to say the least and cause us severe strain. A tarp hanging on a bamboo frame provides shelter from the rain but not the heat. It doesn't screen the zillion insects buzzing my ears while I rest on my cot, a bed without sheets. My boudoir is rustic with dirt floors, tin cans for storage, cardboard boxes for shelves and orange crates for tables. The homey touches are my pictures. I only find solitude when I stand in a trench with a flashlight, the best place to write. My fabulous new uniform is in tatters. I'd leave it on the battlefield if there was anything else to wear. I've lost many personal belongings, but not my wristwatch, as we move from camp to camp like pioneers.

But our ordeal is nothing compared to

what our men tolerate. They bear everything---malaria, semi-starvation, extreme exhaustion, shell shock, shrapnel and bullet wounds, burns from explosions, bombs and anything else the enemy can drop on our heads. Rescues are tough when the Japanese shine searchlights and shell us with artillery when they spot us. Once, we narrowly escaped capture, a story I'll wait to tell over a beer at the Devils. Navy sea planes that have landed in the bay try to protect us, but the Japs have all kinds of opposing fire to pound us with. They are not deterred.

We pray every day for a convoy that's not far away to come and supply relief. We all have one thought in common, end this damn thing. Get us off this old volcano and take us the hell home. Everyone is united around that.

Do you remember that I had never ridden on an airplane before my practice flight? Well, it hasn't exactly been smooth sailing. Air sickness is a real thing. After a few pukes, I learned to control my nausea by swallowing hard and breathing deeply. That seems to have solved the problem, I haven't experienced a bout of it since perfecting my technique. But, boy, was it rough going on those first flights!!

Jeeps take me from the base hospital to open air medical camps near the front. I watch the war up close, just behind the line. Attacks come at us out of the blue. We never know what to expect. We race between the crescendos of battles, standing for twelve-eighteen hours, seeing a hundred patients a day.

We take bets on everything, even how we're going to capture Hirohito. It takes my mind off the limbs we're severing and the holes in chests we're probing, searching for sharp pieces of metal.

I negotiate with mules, monkeys and lizards to walk into the hospital and begin another extraordinary day. Cockroaches as big as mice fly like bats and smack into me, while I'm busy stepping over rats. Sanitation is difficult in this filth, most everyone has a fungus of some kind. Much equipment is rigged up from something else, like the field oven we use to bake our surgical instruments in to sterilize them.

When we're short beds, we remove the box springs from another patient, cover them with blankets and pretend it's a mattress. Some patients lay on the ground when we max out the capacity of our overflowing hospital. We have eight operating tables that stay constantly full. Each man needs a flight out, many are near death, some have their fingers cut off by the Japs who steal their gold wedding rings. All are dirty and sick with disease.

We do our best to distract our patients from their pain and fear. Some of our gals are most entertaining with their many talents. The army nurses in service here have agreed our theme song is the one we wrote, a parody of the Missouri Waltz, which makes me especially happy and homesick. We sing that goofy song to keep us calm.

I can't tell you how strong my hankering is for some of that amazing Kentucky barbecue after a steady ration of fish, rice, dehydrated eggs, and my personal favorite, corned beef hash, cold from the can. When I start to complain, I think of my guys and their predicament, and my troubles fade away. In the field, they barely get one meal a day, some days not even that.

They tell us their secrets or cry out from trauma and shock, then repay us by reciting chirpy little poems and ditties, when they feel better. We reach immediate intimacy when we read the "Dear John" letters sent from their girlfriends, or worse still, their wives. Some have not heard from anyone, including mothers and fathers. They're the ones who really hurt, when I tell them, "No mail today".

Most are decent guys doing what they must to get through this, who defer to me when I do my job. None of this is easy, but no one tries to make it harder. Everyone pitches in for the common good, except for a handful of pompous, demanding senior officers, who assume we will quiver as we stand in awe of them. Some employ poor practices, requiring me to frequently bite my tongue and use diplomacy and tact, two qualities I'm not known for, to avoid correcting a superior.

The exclusive members of this club would never have noticed us in Louisville but regard us well here, because we're American nurses. We're as respectful as mannequins while we listen to them expound on every subject. They value us first as women, then as nurses, until they're shot. Then their bleeding takes precedence over their egos. Fortunately, there are only a few like that, and the nurses know the names of each one. Most of them faint at the sight of blood, so they aren't awake to tell me how to mend them.

I have not found Van, have not found anyone who knows Van, have no new info about him. I listen to the shortwave radio every chance I get to hear news on the back channels. The radiohead has been a big help. He sets me up with headphones, so I know a little about what goes on in the world, while I remain stuck in this god-forsaken place. Not much sounds good, does it? But there is nowhere else I'd rather be. It's the closest I can get to Van. I won't quit looking until I find him.

Ma wrote that Jimmy Moss died somewhere in the Solomons. He lived on our block. We all played together. He and my brother were best friends. I guess this is going to hurt every single one of us, before it's over, isn't it? Looks like we'll both be busy for a good long while. Keep those new recruits coming our way. We sure can use them.

Sending my love to you, dear friend,
Elizabeth Abigail Kizer

Her full name, her prim signature, proving she's still here, still claiming her space, her rightful place.

REUNION

Chapter Fifteen

You must do the thing you think you cannot do.

ELEANOR ROOSEVELT

✿ ✿ ✿

Volunteers from the Crescent Hill Woman's Club decorated a century old farmhouse at Bowman Field and set up a library. They painted the walls a rich cream color and hung blue gingham curtains over the long windows. Members lined shelves with books, many collected from the elegant brick homes of Louisville residents during their Victory Book Drive.

A mill in Knoxville, TN had harvested, dried and shipped mahogany lumber to the vocational education teachers at the high school. The senior boys built shelves, desks and chairs in the wood shop and raced to grab the wheel on the tractor that would pull the load to the library, delivering all but one desk before opening day.

This morning in the library, men were dozing on the donated couches, resting their heads on pillows matching the newly sewn slipcovers. Others read or continued conversations in the comfortable leather chairs. A pack of cards and stacks of poker chips sat waiting on a table set for four. A lone fellow leaned over a long rectangular desk, brow furrowed, pencil paused over paper, thinking through the story he wanted to tell the folks back home.

A lamp with a stained-glass shade in a bright floral pattern lit a dark corner where the historical photographs, donated by the Filson Society, hung in neat rows. They depicted sights around Louisville through the ages---horses standing in the sun at the end of a race, sweat dripping from their flesh or evaporating in the air; aviator Charles Lindbergh visiting Bowman Field; barges navigating winter ice in the Ohio River. More guys lounged there, thumbing through magazines with pictures showing a Turkish bath and the best spots to go fly fishing. When they tore out the photos of the pretty girls for their pinups, Miss Vernon, the librarian, took the mutilated magazines, cut out the remaining pictures and displayed them for all to see.

With their bake sale profits, the indomitable members of the Woman's Club bought the radio for off-duty men and women to gather around and listen to the war reports on the CBS Evening News. Following that and the Lucky Strike jingle, the local WAVE radio station played popular tunes like *Stormy Weather* and *Oh! What a Beautiful Morning*". In this haven, there were no "Quiet" signs, or "No Smoking" signs. Guests made themselves at home, so it was.

Miss Vernon served as both a helpful technician and charming hostess. She edited letters for the men, and wrote them, listened to their troubles and bought birthday presents for mothers and girlfriends, if someone asked her to. Her library, as she saw it, would be a welcoming sanctuary. Her mission was to personally make sure everyone got whatever they requested. Researcher, counselor, tutor, literary advisor, she'd find books they wanted on any subject, from prenatal care to construction techniques, that were as current as those read in universities. For those who found solace there, the library was a poignant reminder of all they missed, a symbol of the hours they had sat on their own front porches with a book, talking to a friend and watching the world walk by. This would be the right place for Jeff's reunion with Jen.

Miss Vernon sat at the front desk keeping a watchful eye from her catbird seat. Colleen approached. "Miss Vernon," she began, clearing a catch in her throat, "May I please ask a favor?"

"Certainly, Nurse O'Brien," she said, reading

the name badge. "What can I do for you?"

"I have a pilot; his name is Captain Jeff Winters. He was badly injured, burned, and he still has a lot of scarring. His girlfriend, Jenny, will visit next weekend. It will be an emotional meeting. I'm looking for a nice place where they can have some privacy. Do you have something for them here?"

"Oh, my dear, of course I do. Come with me." She led Colleen down the hall and opened a door to a small room holding two rocking chairs, a small table with a lamp and a stack of books. "How would this do? Private enough?"

"Yes, perfect. I'll get Jeff here by 1545 on Saturday. Jen's due to arrive around 1600. He's extremely worried about this meeting, her reaction. I want it to go well."

"Certainly. Bring him in through the backdoor. I'll look for you and make sure to keep this hallway empty so you won't be disturbed."

"Thank-you, you're a big help. And Miss Vernon, don't be shocked by what you see. Captain Winters doesn't look like himself yet. We'll show him we're ok with that."

"I understand, Nurse. We'll make sure his first visit to the Bowman Field Library is a good one."

Colleen had added an extra shift at Nichols so she could prepare Jeff for his first meeting with Jen. She went to his room, and he was anxious. "She can't see me like this," he said in despair. "I'm a freak. My face makes a hornet seem sweet. She'll never be able to look at me again. She'll never be able to love me." An involuntary cry escaped from deep within his chest as she examined his tender flesh.

Colleen started the painful process of treating his burns and dug deep inside to withstand her wrenching gut. She forced back the upset that naturally rose in her throat as she surveyed the damage. "Jenny is aware of your injuries, Jeff, and she wants to see you. Give her that chance, and yourself, too."

"I wish I could. Having her to love might be enough to make me want to live again, but how can I ask anyone to commit to a life of caring for me? I'll never be normal, like my old self."

"I don't know, but you can't determine what's best unless you meet with Jen and talk to her about it. Do that and see what happens."

"A look of utter disgust will flash on her exquisite face as she turns away in panic. That's what will happen."

"If you really want me to, Jeff, I can make sure Jenny does not see you, though she has come a very long way. You must be a lonely man without her. Is that what you want?"

"You have no idea how lonely I am. My life has so little value, even to me. It's the loneliest I've ever been, Nurse O'Brien. But I have no right to ask her, or anyone else, to take on this load. It is mine alone."

"Jeff, I've watched you bear this with such

dignity, such valor. You're a brave man. You and Jen might have to start fresh somehow, to figure things out, but you have the courage within you to find a way, if you choose to."

"I want to. I really do want to see her. I've missed her so much and I have to know, but damn, this could be a huge mistake. I'm as scared as a fly in a glue pot. If she takes one look and walks away, well---I don't think I can handle much more disappointment."

"Take it easy. Don't focus on something that hasn't even happened. We'll get you through this. She's traveled far, all the way from Dallas, to be with you. She's lonely for you, too. She may be shocked at first glance, but once you talk, she'll recognize you're the man she loves. Give her the space and time to trust that love and think her way through this a little bit. It's all new to her."

"Why should my beautiful Jen give up everything in her life for me? She can have any guy she wants. I'll only be good for hollerin' down the well."

"She wants you."

"She wanted me. The old me. The one who still had a face. And a future. What do I have to give her now?"

Colleen paused to look at Jeff directly, to absorb the depth of what he was feeling. It was no wonder he had drawn that conclusion. This dreadful war had taken everything from him, as it had so many others. His sadness at such a devastating loss threatened to overcome her, as it had him. Finding the silver lining seemed impossible, indeed.

"Come on," she said, forcing herself to dispel those thoughts and complete the ablution for the day. "Let's get you in your Sunday best. After you're fresh as a daisy, I'll move you out of here and into a lovely room at the library, where you can receive Jenny in private."

He did not resist as Colleen changed him into clean, loose-fitting clothes, adjusted his IVs and gently placed a baseball cap on the bandages wrapped around his head. The plastic surgeons had performed a miracle, surgically reforming a stump with a hole into something akin to a nose and reshaping his face, crafted from a transplanted bone. The skin grafts on his flaming red flesh were raw but healing, the scars fading ever so slightly.

From a distance and the correct angle, the right side of his face looked like Jeff's on the body of a frail, but whole, man. His eye was still the clearest green, a dimple still creased his cheek. With a slight turn of his head, however, the front view showed the restructured nose and a cheek beneath melted flesh. Layers of skin still sagged in folds, one on top of the other in streaks of brown and sizzling red. Across his forehead and around his eyes, skin stretched as taut as a mast in full sail, drawing his expression into something an alien might wear.

It was unreasonable to ignore what was so

plainly visible. In order to control her reaction, Colleen thought through the inevitable feelings that surfaced whenever she looked at Jeff. Not revulsion or disgust, but shock and dismay, when she remembered the attractive guy who hugged her his last night at Bowman. How could she describe for Jen the severity of his disfigurement? How could she expect Jen to be ok with it?

She had spent hours at the bedside of this weakened and tormented man, aiding in his care, knowing and loving him. She affirmed he is the same gentle Jeff who walked her home that fraught evening a couple of months ago. How could she convince Jen that so much of him was still the same?

His life is irrevocably changed, how will he find a will to live? How can I help him transition to his new, and decidedly different, life? How can I help Jen see the person she loves still breathes in his body? Will she see the courage we witness as he struggles with the next gasp? How can Jen channel her despair over what he's lost? Over what she's lost? When she looks into a hole where there is no eye, a mouth that cannot chew, a nose that wheezes air through paper-thin skin, shaped like clay onto something barely resembling a visage her friends back home could identify? How can she offer a genuine smile to show her acceptance of that?

Jeff sat nervously in his wheelchair in the library's parlor, his back to the door. Colleen stood just outside in the hallway, waiting for the tall, lovely woman to approach. Jen was as attractive as Jeff had claimed.

"Miss Welch?" Colleen asked, extending her hand.

"Yes, I'm Jenny Welch. The librarian told me I would find Jeff here?"

"He's inside this room."

"Oh, thank God. May I see him, please?" Jen reached for the door handle.

"Wait," said Colleen, "before you go in, you should know what to expect."

"I know his face is burned, right? But he's still Jeff, my Jeff, isn't he?"

"Yes, yes, he is your Jeff. Perhaps you don't realize the severity of his injuries. His face is quite distorted."

"Don't worry about me, Nurse. I'll be just fine. Please, let me see him."

Colleen opened the door and she and Jenny stepped through. Jen ran to him, calling his name, falling to her knees at his feet, her head in his lap, her face full of tears.

He placed his hands on her head and stroked her hair, "Oh, Jen, my beautiful Jen, oh, Jen," he repeated.

Colleen watched as two full minutes of sobbing passed before Jen raised her head to look at his face in full view. She gasped when she understood the truth of what she saw, a man barely distinguishable as her beloved Jeff. She averted her face, could not look, could not take it in. Colleen's heart sank as she interpreted Jen's reaction.

Jeff also saw her expression and stopped inhaling, his lungs too deflated to pump oxygen. His breath paused in that moment. He wondered if it was worth it to will his lungs to keep pushing air. Maybe he should let them go dormant forever.

"Oh, Jeff, I didn't realize, I'm so sorry, my darling," she said, barely lifting her eyes to see. "What have they done to you, what have they done?" she wailed.

"It's my fault, Jen," he chuckled, "I didn't move fast enough, I guess."

"Nurse," Jen said, turning to Colleen, who stood close behind Jeff's chair. "What can we do to help him? There must be something."

Colleen rested her hand on his shoulder to steady him. "I assure you, Jenny, he is receiving the best medical care available. His injuries are severe. We don't know how long healing will take. The doctors saved his life. Surgeons have started to rebuild his face, but he has a rigorous road ahead. There is no easy path for him, or you, if you join him on it."

"Jen, you don't have to. I know what I look like. This isn't what you signed up for. From now on, I'll be about as useless to you as a skunk at a lawn party. I don't presume you'll stick by me. It's enough that you didn't forget me entirely and cared enough to come here today."

"Jeffrey Reynolds Winters, what are you talking about?" Jen said, rising to her feet and looking astonished. She leaned toward him, stopping when her face was directly opposite his, in full, close-up view of his injuries. "Of course, I intend to stick with you, if you'll have me. I love you, my darling, nothing changes that." She rested her head on his chest and he bent over her. With humility and gratitude, he embraced her and all the love she gave him, returning it tenfold.

Colleen smiled. "It looks like you two have much to talk about, so I'll leave you alone for a while," she said. "Take as long as you like. If you need me, Jeff, you know where to find me."

"Nurse O'Brien has been a terrific help to me, Jen, you'll never know how much. But I think we've got this," he said in Colleen's direction. He was so overcome with emotion he could barely complete the sentence. He conveyed his thanks without words.

"We sure do, Nurse O'Brien," Jen said softly, still looking at him.

Colleen waved and walked through the door. *Jenny Welch is as wonderful as Jeff bragged that she was the night we met. This is the best story I will tell from the war. Not everyone gets a happy ending, but I'm glad they did. How does anyone get so fortunate to have a love like theirs? Will I ever find out?*

The only thing that could make her day more memorable was delivering a baby. That's just what she did. After completing her shift, she returned to the barracks for a solid night of rest before meeting students at 0800. However, she was paged at 0230 and asked to return to Nichols at once.

She dressed quickly and ran the distance. The night nurse sounded panicked. She was as solid as an ox, so Colleen knew something must be terribly wrong. She arrived and checked in on the patient as directed. She found a woman deep in labor; things clearly were not progressing well. A floor full of bloody gauze reflected a hectic scene. The doctor on duty bore a bit of a quizzical expression. His practice delivering newborns was limited, and this birth was complicated. Twin bodies pressed to enter the world, but nothing was happening. Both mother and babies were waning.

Colleen walked to the mother's head and realized she looked familiar. The sheriff's wife. She leaned closely into her face and whispered, "Mrs. Hamilton, I'm going to take good care of you. You're going to deliver two healthy babies in just a few minutes. Please trust me now, we'll get this done very soon."

Doctor Tubman looked relieved when she appeared to take charge. She assessed the situation and quickly repositioned mother and doctor so both could co-operate better. Colleen measured her dilation at ten centimeters. She checked her vitals.

"We must act quickly. The babies are stressed. I will use my hands to turn and pull out baby number one. Be ready to grab him when he pops."

The doctor held a large, clean towel. Colleen inserted her gloved hands far enough to feel the baby's contour. At that moment, the power went out. The room became dark.

"Good heavens," she said. "We can't deliver her without light. Someone please find a flashlight." Turning to Mrs. Hamilton she said, "We can't wait. Push now, Evelyn. Push, push," she said.

Evelyn screamed as Colleen carefully tugged and turned until the baby's bottom and one arm plopped out, but the rest remained stuck. With greater force she pulled and wriggled the infant, until suddenly the child fell directly into Doctor Tubman's towel. He rubbed her chest with his finger, and the newborn let out a boisterous cry.

Colleen returned her attention to Mrs. Hamilton. In the dim light she saw that Evelyn was in great distress. Her blood pressure rocketed up; her speech sounded slurred.

"We've got to deliver this baby immediately," Colleen said to the doctor. "We're getting this baby out of you, Evelyn. When I ask you to push, give it all you've got. Ok. Come on, push as hard as you can."

Evelyn Hamilton couldn't find the energy to accommodate and fell back on the bed, completely used up.

"You can't rest yet, Evelyn. We're going to deliver your baby. We both have a job to do. I'm going to pull and you're going to push. We'll get it done right now, and you'll have two blessed babes to cherish, ok? Push with every ounce of strength you can find! Now!"

Evelyn was barely cognizant of anyone else in the room but responded to the urgent plea in Colleen's voice. She let out one last, feral scream and contracted her muscles with a powerful flex. Colleen grabbed the child and pulled, turning and twisting as she did so. The tiny girl slid into her waiting arms, looking at her through shining half-moon slits and a sucking motion parting her lips. She gurgled she was hungry for breakfast and ready for a warm bath.

Colleen handed her to the other nurse to clean, then tested the newborns for any abnormalities, while Doctor Tubman attended to Mrs. Hamilton. Her pressure normalized and she leaned back on her pillows, smiling and swallowing small sips of juice. Colleen placed two daughters, one after the other, on their mother's breasts, cajoling them until they each latched on. She left the delivery room three hours before her next class confident in her expertise, exhausted but exultant, her sins expunged for a day.

REVELATION

Chapter Sixteen

*No one can make you feel inferior
without your consent.*

ELEANOR ROOSEVELT

❉ ❉ ❉

On Sunday, her day off, Colleen clocked in at Nichols at 0700. She always said "yes" when the workload required Captain Chantel to schedule her for an additional shift, an assignment she welcomed. She enjoyed being with patients. While teaching her class and graduating the students rewarded her devotion, it didn't satisfy her mission to use her hands to heal.

The first person she checked on was Jeff, who dedicated every day to his laborious and harrowing, but steady, recovery, due in part to Jen's constant encouragement. Soon he would be well enough to return to Texas with her. She remained by his side, committed to him. Together they would navigate the years ahead enduring his reconstructive surgeries.

"Any mail for me?" he asked, like every other man she would visit during her shift.

"Sorry, no," came her reply, the same that she gave to most of those who asked.

For the men in the ward, the highlight of their days was to receive a letter from their girlfriends or wives and to hear the town's gossip from Mom or Dad. Mail was slow to catch up with them, but a package of oranges arrived yesterday and dates today. Although it was a food not normally savored as a treat, dates could travel many miles and remain edible until they reached their destination. The men relished each delicious nugget.

They devoured postcards that were three months old and copies of Stars and Stripes full of history, not news. They wanted to know, "Do they really have gas rationing in Minnesota?" "Is it true you can't buy coffee in the grocery store?"

"I can't even consider Broadway being blacked out," the boys from New York said, holding old copies of the Times. "The speed limit is 35 mph now, Walter," Scott shouted across the room, as Walter shook his head in disbelief. "They say there is no traffic in Iowa, because there is no rubber for tires," he added.

"Who are the top baseball players this season?" Harry wanted to know, but the statistics listed were out of date. "What's the latest song by Vera Lynn?" asked Calvin. "Since I heard her on the BBC, I'm her number one fan." They celebrated or cursed who won the hometown high school football game opposite their rival. Most of all, they asked if their folks realized what it's like over there. Do they read about what happened to the buddies they left behind? Do they grieve for their brothers dying beside them in the foxhole? The ones who did not make it out?

They liked reading that people bought quotas of war bonds to provide supplies for them, that volunteers donated pints of blood for transfusions and spent long hours in service at the Red Cross. They could not yet imagine their sisters and mothers filling the jobs they formerly did, or the ones at the new war production plant making military equipment they use on the battlefields. The photographs of women wearing coveralls and tool belts, welding bolts on airplane wings, didn't convince them. That could not be real.

Colleen handed a letter to one young soldier who had started out in the Solomons and transferred to Bowman recently from a Canadian hospital. Corporal Tyson Keaton, who left Ohio more than two years ago, was thrilled to be on American soil at last. He signaled a desire to talk; Colleen slowly changed his bandages to give him the opportunity.

"On the first flight out to the base hospital on Guadalcanal," he said, "when I came to and saw that good-looking nurse, I thought, 'Good lord, it's a woman,' and hailed her queen. None of us guys ever saw anything but dogfaces since we left home, so everyone was glad to see her. If they could, they joined me in treating her like royalty the whole way back. Not that we could do much strapped to the wall of an airplane. But through that long, terrible trip, we did our best to lighten her load. I want to personally thank her. How can I do that?"

"That nurse doesn't expect anything from you, Corporal Keaton. If she saved your life and risked hers to do it, it's a commitment she chose. The nurses know you appreciate what they do for you."

"She's my hero."

"They are patriots, just like you."

"Yeah, well I sure would like to see her once more," he groaned, as she rolled him on his side, "to make sure she wasn't something I dreamed up."

Colleen took scissors and cut the tape off a bandage that wrapped from his chest to his spine. "I sure would like to see her just once," he repeated. "I hafta' thank her for being the guardian angel who came to my rescue. My carcass would be rotting in that jungle sun, if she hadn't come along right when I needed her."

"We aim to please. If she was a U. S. air evac nurse, she trained right here at Bowman Field. Do you remember her name?"

"I'll never forget it. Her badge read:

Second Lieutenant Elizabeth Kizer, RN
U. S. Army Air Evacuation Corps"

"Liz was your nurse? She's my friend! Tell me, please, how is she?"

"Oh, man, she's super. Never stopped moving, always helping somebody. We started to worry about *her*. Nurse Elizabeth sure had the touch."

"How long ago did you see her?"

"I don't know, miss, but it's been a while. After she patched me up, I spent a few weeks in the base hospital before moving on to Canada and then here. Hell, I've lost track of time, I don't know what day it is."

"It's Friday, August 27, 1943. We'll get you to the library soon, so you can read the paper and catch up. Do you know where Liz was going next?"

"Nah, all I know is I never saw her eat or take a break. She was too busy talking to the soldiers. One guy was shot, and she was hanging blood bags. Another couldn't breathe, she pumped air. Somebody else screamed in pain. Everyone called for her. One way or another, I gotta' find her, so I can thank her in person for saving me...."

His speech faded as his body gave out. Colleen checked his pulse, completed treating his wounds, wrapped a new bandage around his chest, hung fresh IVs bulging with fluids and prepared him, and the room, for rest. Corporal Keaton's passion for Liz was keeping him alive.

She tended to her final patient and delivered the last envelope before returning the mail cart to the base post office, lining it up next to the others. As she pivoted to leave, Corporal Martin, the temporary mailroom supervisor, called to her. He had noticeably improved the efficiency of the postal service in the four months since his assignment. She was sorry to learn that he would be sent overseas soon.

"Nurse O'Brien, I've got a letter here for ya'," he called to her.

"Oh, how exciting, Corporal Martin," she said, walking toward him to receive the envelope. "Say, I heard you're flying out of here next week. Is that true?"

"'Fraid so. It's my turn, I guess."

"Well, I'll miss seeing you. You've done such a nice job with our little postal department."

"Thank you, Nurse. I'll miss my customers. It always made me feel good to deliver mail to them. They were so glad to see me. Sorry I couldn't give this one to you earlier," he said, handing it over. "It wasn't sorted yet."

"That's ok, Corporal Martin," she said, glancing at the address. Instantly, it eviscerated her. Tommy's big, bold script was unmistakable. Seeing it caused a feeling of powerlessness to wash over her. A little too suddenly, she wished the Corporal well and dashed from the building. Walking quickly, head down, she started to read.

Hey baby,

Your Mama gave me your address when I saw
Chloe on Sunday. She only lets me see Chloe in
her parlor. This whole thing is messed up, Colleen.
I demand you come home and straighten things
out. You know you're the only girl for me and we
belong together. No one deserves you like I do. I
treat you good, gorgeous girl, because I love you.
We have fun, remember the night on Dead Man's
Hill? That's what counts. I've always had a temper.
You know that. It might get the best of me once
in a while. I promise it won't happen again and
I will make it up to you. But you were wrong to
spend money without asking, and worse still for
sassing back. Stop talking when I say so because
your whining doesn't help. No matter what, you
have no right to walk out. I give you everything
you need and take care of my girls. I won't hold
this against you, if you come home right now. You
belong in Ithaca, not half a country away. Let's fix
this, so we can be a family again, together in our
own house.

I saw Father O'Malley at Flanagan's. He heard you
left and he said your obligation is here. Do you
remember his advice before our wedding? Well,
now would be a real good time to follow it. Your
Mama and Papa want you home, that's a fact. They
do not want you in KY. What about Chloe? Do you

think you're a good mother when you're not even here? I don't, and your sister and mine agree with me. So does Veronica. No one understands how you left our little girl to go on some wild goose chase so far from us. Come home, Colleen, or I WILL get pissed.

Your loving husband,
Thomas O'Brien

Colleen scrunched the letter into a ball and held it close to her pounding chest. She could picture him hunched over the kitchen table, scratching words on paper. The image of him there, in the center of her home, in front of her hearth, filled her with revulsion, not warmth.

Why do I react like this? About a letter from Tommy? Why does it upset me so? Her face burned red. *He told Father O'Malley I left him? He talked to Sarah and Veronica about me? Did he tell everyone we know? Well, I shouldn't be surprised, should I? Of course, Tommy would talk. To everyone. What did I expect?*

In a small community, everyone talks about everyone's business. They all would have plenty to say about her situation. Tommy was right that Mama would worry. She already knew Papa didn't want her there. He'd said that much to her directly, before she parted from them. Tommy was also right that wives do not walk out on husbands, mothers do not abandon daughters, based on flimsy instincts.

But Mama had understood her compulsion to start over. She had lived her own adventure when she was a young woman, after running away from home when a love affair ended sadly. She told her children that living in New York City, writing and taking photos for the Irish Times, was an exciting and interesting year in her life. She never regretted it and always said she was glad she did it. The Times eventually sent her to Galveston, Texas to report on the 1900 hurricane. While there, she met the formidable Miss Clara Barton, who was completing her final mission. That changed everything for Mama.

Mama may wish me to come home, but she did not prevent me from leaving. My husband knocked me to the floor, putting our daughter and me in danger. It was the need to be safe, to be respected, that propelled me out that door with Chloe in one hand and my medical bag in the other. That was the price I paid for us to survive.

It was fear and despair and indignation about what was, and a persistent belief in what could be, that had brought her here. Still....

As usual, somehow Tommy O'Brien had gotten to her. Why did conversations with him, even those via pencil and paper, cause her throat to constrict and her stomach to flutter? Why did she struggle to get the words out when she tried to defend her actions? Why did she have to defend her actions? Wasn't she a mature woman, able to think for herself? How was it that her husband caused her to clam up, to remain silent? To lose confidence in her own abilities?

At the Sunday dinner at the O'Brien's, when she had asked Father O'Malley why women couldn't become ordained priests, Tommy had said, "You can't be serious! Women priests?" and started to laugh at the mere idea of it. His brothers and father joined in the heckling. Mrs. O'Brien gave her a look that said "shush". As Colleen's cheeks blistered with humiliation, she vowed to never again give any of them an opportunity to demean her. Thereafter, she guarded her words in their presence.

Yet there were other incidents, too. That day in the garden, the predicament at church. She blushed remembering the Christmas party. She had been styling her hair in a chignon as she dressed for the evening. Chloe fell and injured her knee, and she took time to clean the wound and calm Chloe with a kiss. She forgot the three curls still bobby-pinned on the back of her head and walked happily to the party at Tommy's side. When she returned home later that evening, she discovered the three clips still holding the strands of flattened curls. They remained pinned against her neck above the elegant ruffles that lined the party frock she'd sewn especially for the holidays. She cringed with embarrassment. *How ridiculous I must have looked! Why didn't Tommy tell me?*

"Good God, Colleen, don't you think you're

making too big a deal out of this?" Tommy had said as she held the mirror up to look. "I mean, who cares? I didn't even notice your hair was full of pins."

"That's the point, Tommy," she said, "you didn't even notice!"   The only comfort Tommy could offer was that, maybe, no one else did, either.

Soon after, she bought the vaporizer for Chloe without permission, and that was that.

It occurred to her that others did not speak to her as Tommy did. In fact, they behaved differently toward her, too. The reactions of her patients and colleagues reflected their dependence on her, their faith in her good will and competence. She'd earned their esteem and they responded accordingly.

The men on 3B didn't roll their eyes when she greeted them and treated their wounds. They thanked her for good care. They flirted and teased and commiserated. They did not disdain.

The women taking her class and training during bivouac did not ignore her comments. They listened as if their survival hung on them.

Jeff heard her words and often said how much he valued her direction regarding his care. More to the point, he honored her words by obeying them, showing he relied on that direction.

She relished her relationship with Liz. It was one of mutual respect. Liz sought her counsel and valued her advice. When they disagreed, Liz did not use words to degrade her. She used words to settle the issue.

Every mother in labor and delivery took her advice, soothed by her disciplined concern, never calling out in doubt when she commanded them to push.

Her parents probably adored her every utterance. With them, she never guarded her words. They encouraged her honesty.

How about the butcher? During their first year of marriage, when money was tight and she promised to pay, didn't he extend credit to her family based on her word alone? And didn't she pay him each week as agreed? Why couldn't Tommy trust her at least as much as Mr. Neufelder?

Not everyone valued what she said, of course. The Church showed little interest in the views of women. She treasured the sacredness, beauty and history of the Church, the rituals and music, the extraordinary art and architecture. She loved the community she'd known since birth. But she didn't much care what the patriarchy had to say. The Church's exclusive board of directors spoke for men, not her, she had concluded, sitting in Sister Mary Dorothy's catechism class. She realized that if she could not participate fully within the established power structure, if she could not have an equal voice and cast a vote, she wasn't much interested in the decisions made by the pope, the bishops and the priests. Until things changed, she and the Church were, regretfully, at an impasse. But not for long. *Now that women have achieved suffrage, the Church will grant women equal authority very soon. Some will even become priests! It's only a matter of time. Thank God, there are infinite ways to worship, until then.*

Most of her teachers had exemplified their roles as information providers, and she understood her role as a student. Most ignored her and did not seek her opinions, but she didn't harbor hard feelings on that score. They treated all women the same, not just her, as well as many of the men. Things could have been much worse. She could have been denied an education altogether and was willing to accept that status quo in order to receive one.

Why is it that only Tommy O'Brien silences me in ways that no one else can? Through a thousand slender slights? That's just how it is, I've always said. Well, to hell with that!

Previously, she tried to shrug off these rumblings. They would lead to trouble. They did not merit her consideration. She had plenty to think about with Chloe and work. But, here, suddenly, something seemed different, like she'd had a revelation of sorts. It was only Tommy O'Brien who ridiculed her, or rolled his eyes with derision when she spoke, or blew her off, or cast a comment that distorted her words, or uttered remarks employed precisely to shut her down. It was only Tommy O'Brien who showed contempt for her. She had seen vivid flashes of that contempt with her own eyes and bore the results of it on her jaw.

How did I miss this? How did I not understand it for what it was? Not recognize the hatred inherent in his actions? The anger alive in those same two hands that held me? I've grown up with him. Is it possible I have become so accustomed to his ways, so accepting, so acquiescing, I can't see him for who he is? Who is he? The man I loved? Or the one who nearly killed me?

Damn it! This was all too confusing. She wanted to write Liz. Liz could explain to her what was happening, could help her sort this out like she always did. But Colleen couldn't impose her troubles on Liz. She did not need this worry. No one did.

Colleen found herself drawn to Jeff's door. She paused without entering, trying to relax her face with a smile. She decided to return to the barracks and not disturb him, but he saw her through the window and motioned her in.

"Two visits in one day? That makes me about as lucky as the guy who always draws the ace," Jeff said, looking closely at her. He saw that she was upset. "Whoa, Colleen, what's going on? You look like you're eating sorrow by the spoonful. Are you alright?"

"I received a letter from Tommy. He wants me to come home. I don't know what to do."

"How many months ago did we meet, Colleen? Six? You know most everything about me, don't you? We've been pretty truthful with each other, haven't we? No secrets?"

She nodded and sighed, waiting for him to make his point.

"Then I'm going to state the obvious to you now. You can't charge into hell with only a bucket of ice water."

"I don't know what you mean, Jeff."

"Listen, Colleen. Your only goal has been to make a safe home for you and Chloe, right? That's your reason for being here, and it's a good one. From what you've told me about Tommy, he's got a ten-gallon mouth and a temper that's as big as half of Texas. It's dangerous for you there. Even a dead snake can still bite, and that snake still lives."

"I have to go home some time. I can't stay away from Chloe much longer."

"When does your commitment to the Army expire?"

"My year is up in March," she said, filling his cup with water and straightening his sheets.

"Then don't blow the Triple Crown by betting on the wrong horse. You've got a heart as big as Dallas, and you came here all set to find a means to an end. Find it. Find it, so you can take care of yourself. Find it so you can decide if the father of your daughter can be trusted with her. Find it so you can choose to live in peace.

"But Tommy is my husband. And Chloe's daddy. I can't deny that."

"He is, but any guy who would put his fist on you is so low he'd have to look up to see dirt. That's who Tommy is. He doesn't deserve you, or Chloe. You cannot stay with him, can you? I mean, is that what you want?"

Colleen looked at him, amazed at how well he understood her, how well he could get to the root of any problem. She valued his honesty the most, and the kindness he showed her.

"I want Chloe and me to breathe free."

"If you believe that to be true, you must live it, or you will live a lie. You can't be complicit any longer. Your daughter is the deepest part of you. Protect her. Don't waste your time on a guy who's all hat and no horse."

"I don't know the best way to protect Chloe. Doesn't she need her father, too? I don't think I can do everything by myself. I don't know if I want to."

"Boy, you really don't see yourself as others see you, Colleen. You're as tough as any gal on the ranch and as fine as my Momma's cream gravy. But you've got a yellow jacket in your outhouse and you won't admit it. You have a right to live without fear. You have a right to be who you are without fear."

"That's what I want for my daughter."

"Then trust your intuition, you'll figure out what to do."

"It scares me to go it alone."

"You'll learn real quick how to skin your own buffalo. When you do, your soul may feel like it's worn a little thin at times, but it'll be a little wiser, too."

"I sure wish I could be certain of that."

"You can hang your hat on it, Colleen. Look, I can explain this to you, but I can't make you believe it. All I know is, I see a woman who is living her dream to become a better nurse and make a better life for her child. That's the sway you hold, Colleen. It's born of your love for Chloe and your personal courage. It's a win-win. Let it shape you. Let it change your attitude. Let it bring your glory out. You deserve to be as happy as a hog in mud, but you won't be if your life is threatened by the very man who is supposed to care for you."

She reached out to touch his hand. "You make me sound so grand." She worked to hold back poignant tears of both gratitude and sadness.

Jeff shifted in his bed to look at her directly. "You are grand, Colleen, that's it exactly. Ask yourself, can you live with a guy who shoots craps with the devil himself? If you can't, build a wall tall enough he can't climb over it."

"How do I do that?"

"Just like you tell me to do every day, my friend, through the force of your own will, your own magical thinking. State clearly your most fervent desire, imagine the best and foster your future, day after day."

Colleen leaned in for a sweet kiss and left him resting. She returned to the barracks and placed Tommy's letter under her pillow. She climbed into bed late that night, aware that, because of Jeff, she had walked through the forest and grown taller than the redwoods. She did not have to accept what others expected her to do. What Tommy expected her to do. Jeff was right. She could take care of herself and Chloe. She had mastered that skill. She was already doing it.

NEWS

Chapter Seventeen

*This generation of Americans has
a rendezvous with destiny.*

PRESIDENT FRANKLIN D. ROOSEVELT

❊ ❊ ❊

Colleen made it a habit to visit the library on her way back to the barracks after class, when she wasn't answering Captain Chantel's call to work the late shift at Nichols. Sharing space with like-minded service men and women provided meaningful connections among them all. The esprit de corps was palpable. As the others read, talked or played games, she settled into the chair with the comfy embroidered pillows, a copy of the Courier-Journal in hand. Miss Vernon set up a conducive environment and encouraged guests to rest. Colleen was happy to oblige. She'd stay long enough to read the daily war report. If she found an interesting article or two, she might stay in her cozy confines a little longer.

It was there she read the latest news...about Liz! A grainy picture on the front page of the paper showed a nurse leaning over an injured soldier lying on the ground. She was tending to his wound, looking at him, not the camera. The photo was fuzzy, but the outline of Liz's profile was unmistakable; that strong nose and perfect square jaw, the curly sprig of hair that popped out uninvited under the brim of her cap.

Colleen read the caption below the picture.

Vella Lavella Island---U.S. Army Air Corps Second Lieutenant Elizabeth Kizer attends a soldier on a beach in the Solomon Islands. He was the last of the twenty-eight patients to be loaded for transport to a base hospital on Guadalcanal. In her capable hands, their healing begins. She expects them all to survive the flight.

War correspondent Charles Dempsey, a colleague of the famous Ernie Pyle, wrote the article. Dempsey described the scene, interviewed Liz and quoted her throughout the piece.

VELLA LAVELLA, SOLOMON ISLANDS---On Sunday, August 29, I arrived before dawn on this rock that's like a fortress, protecting the bay that is the entrance to the island, Vella Lavella. I came to embed with the Americans who fight thirty yards from the trench I'm crouched in.

U.S. sailors on the ships in the bay and soldiers on land vow to continue their assaults on the Japanese despite these unmanageable conditions. They are determined to avenge their comrades who gave their lives in the dense jungles of the Solomons, as they battled to the end. The American doctors and nurses who care for them were overwhelmed after fifteen days and nights of ceaseless fighting that climaxed three months during which the men agonized through the torment of hell.

Japanese troops hammered this war-ravaged and blood-stained land hour after hour. Their dive bombers buzzed overhead through the night. The U.S. Navy acted quickly to support our soldiers, while Japanese tanks and artillery chewed up the fox holes hiding the battered men. They withstood these blows despite the fever, hunger and weariness that racks them and diminishes their strength.

The remnants of this valiant army swam across a two-mile river to a small boat, which they used to reach the nurses on the other side and bring them back to the wounded. Our fighters held off powerful enemy forces while nurses rushed in to save as many as they could.

On Monday, they treated more than a hundred casualties on the field. According to Second Lieutenant Elizabeth Kizer, "There was so much firepower that bodies flew through the air. Shooting came from the planes above as well as forces on the ground. Our guys were sitting ducks. They didn't have a chance to protect themselves, but they stayed at their posts. They are so brave.

"When we wheeled them into the hospital, they said, 'We had to do it, it's what we signed up for.' I get sick when I think about them, their bloody bodies all torn up. Tomorrow will be more of the same."

As war rages on, wounded Americans have fallen on battlefields all over the world. When they come-to, they think they are in heaven, so surprised are they by these welcoming, attractive nurses, the last thing they guessed would be in this land of misery.

The nurses, wearing the gold bars of the Army Air Corps, travel with the troops to set up mobile field hospitals. By early Wednesday morning, it was already hot. The convoy bumped along dirt roads full of potholes, hour after hour with frequent delays. Our trucks rumbled through a small village with a few houses and stores on one main street, between the church on one end and the school on the other.

Women, children and one old man stared at us as we watched them from our vehicles. A priest wearing a threadbare black cassock stood on the steps of his church. When Lieutenant Kissel approached him, Father Jasper Mathias offered his school for our use, since students could no longer attend.

Travel had begun at 0500, but the day was just starting. The staff efficiently removed desks and chairs to make room for a hospital. They set up cots, supplies, a surgery center and recovery ward to care for the first casualties. For the next fourteen hours, there was no let up.

When a company got pinned down on a railroad track, they took heavy losses. Nurses soon arrived and filled every litter with hurting men, until there were no more, then rushed them back to the school. The medical staff stayed awake through the night and following day, until every injury was addressed.

The nuns in the convent, teachers for the school, invited the nurses to stay with them. They rearranged a large storage area for a dormitory for them to sleep. The nurses had lived under tarps covering the tops of trucks that gave little protection from the weather or mosquitoes, so they were delighted to move into the school. They expressed thanks to the nuns for the chance to bed down under a real roof. Twenty-seven war orphans in the nun's care shared the home and slept in similar dormitories, boys in the hallway, girls in the parlor.

The nurses, wearing their overalls and slacks, are not glamour girls. They march with heavy backpacks that almost pull them over. With no other sources of food, these hungry men and women eat k-rations three meals a day. The tasteless scrambled eggs with meat and the canned biscuits they call dog crackers do not remind anyone of Mom's home cooking. Adding some powder to water and mixing it in a tin cup passes for lemonade, the closest thing to a party treat they have.

The elderly convent cook has been sharing her food with them. Before bed, the weary nurses get a big pot of coffee set up for the next morning and put a bucket of coal in the kitchen stove. If no oven fire is set for the cook when she arrives at 0530, she starts one, moving so slowly the nurses miss breakfast.

To bathe, the women gather wood and chop it with an ax until it is small enough to fit in a tiny fire pit found under the water tank. After a lot of effort and ever more patience, a little hot water pours into the tub, which they prefer to use instead of the mountain stream accessed by thousands of others for bathing and laundry.

The hospital remained in this place for six days until the nurses evacuated the patients, airlifting them out for further evaluation and treatment. As quickly as they set it up, they took the hospital down, packing equipment and supplies and getting their personal gear in order. They do this over and over, so it is routine. When the outfit they support rests, they are sent to another one heading into action.

Yesterday, surgeons amputated Nurse Kizer's left arm. She was injured by enemy blasts directed at the hospital. Nurse Kizer waited without complaint while others were given priority medical relief.

Lieutenant Totten said, "The nurses are as good a soldier as you ever saw." These angels of mercy fly on man-made wings, subject to duty anywhere the army sees fit to order them. They could take an easier way, but they stick with their units. They do not waste their opportunities. They live for today.

Last night, a small group of trapped Japanese men touched off the pitiful store of ammunition that remained. The red glare signaled to us they were beaten. This morning, they put down their arms on this desolate island.

Our tired and haggard troops have gathered, and a steady stream, miles-long, are still walking in. Every American should bow in tribute to these valiant G. I. Joes.

Colleen reread the paragraph about Liz and the amputation before throwing the paper in a heap on the floor and running out the door. She wanted to vomit and tried to gulp fresh air but couldn't catch her breath. The realization that Liz had lost an arm started to sink in. *Oh my God! Where is she? How is she? Who is with her? Is she alone? Liz lives to be a nurse. How can she continue without her arm? This job means everything to her, to her whole family. They rely on her. Without it, she will be lost. She could be pushed back into the poverty she's tried so hard to escape. Liz needs me. I must get to her.*

RECOVERY

Chapter Eighteen

*The best luck of all is the luck
you make for yourself.*

GENERAL DOUGLAS MACARTHUR

❊ ❊ ❊

T he following Saturday, Colleen spent twelve
hours with a group of priests and seminarians
from St. Meinrad School of Theology, extracting
more than a hundred pints of donated blood for
the Red Cross. Her mother, Mary Caroline, had told
her stories of the months she volunteered for the
Red Cross after Galveston's great storm. Miss Clara
Barton asked her to set up an orphanage there. It
had become a mother/daughter tradition to aid the
Red Cross. Colleen intended for Chloe to join them
as soon as she was old enough.

It was there that Colleen heard Liz
was returning to Nichols. Captain Chantel
also volunteered that afternoon, where sitting,

drinking tea and chatting with others while rolling bandages and preparing supplies looked like a party. Commander Jolson had told the captain that in the next forty-eight hours, she should anticipate receiving a Bowman nurse, who had been injured in the field. Liz.

It was two days before Colleen could see her. She arrived late Sunday evening on a stretcher and in a coma, then spent the next day with doctors who examined her and nurses who established her treatment regimen.

When Colleen entered the room, she began tending to her friend, her patient. A few hours earlier, Liz had regained consciousness, but remained sedated. Colleen examined her first. She had lived on field rations for months. Colleen saw that her body had thinned to skeleton weight with ribs protruding. Lesions, abrasions and insect bites covered her skin in scabbed or scaly, inflamed patches.

Colleen retrieved Liz's chart to review. Japanese bombs exploding around her, and the rat-ta-tat-tat of rifles in front of her, had punctured her eardrum. The chart stated: "hearing loss, recovery possible".

A huge explosion shattered her left arm below the elbow. Doctors had surgically removed her forearm: "stump wound red, warm, good blood circulation; no infection noted".

The head injury, the most serious of those she'd sustained, heavily bruised the left, rear quadrant of her brain; "probable paralysis of right arm and leg, compromised ability to speak and use language".

The only prescription for this grim diagnosis was to allow brain swelling to subside, continue monitoring and allow time for her to improve. The effects of that kind of damage vary widely from mild to severe, but loss of function seemed inevitable. Often, an injury to the brain cannot be reversed.

Wait and see, that's the best they can do for Liz? That's the best I can do? Hell, no, there was more, and Colleen set about ensuring it got done.

Liz fluttered her eyelids and tried to distinguish who leaned over her. The moment she sensed Colleen's touch, she knew.

"Good afternoon, lovely," Colleen said, seeing that Liz was trying to speak. "So glad to see you're awake. You were in a coma for a few days, very nice of you to wake up."

"Hey, girl," Liz replied weakly, "how are you?" Her voice was sluggish, but she recalled words, an excellent sign.

"I'm fine. The question is, how are you?"

"I've got a headache that, that, that feels like a hammer is pounding a, uh, a nail in the middle of my forehead," she stammered, then paused for a deep breath. "There's a drunk bell choir ringing in my left ear. I can barely hear in the right. Otherwise, I've never been better," she said softly, slowly.

Colleen noted the slowness, the slurring of "r" and "s". "Ok, I get it. Doc says that headache will probably leave you soon, but the good news is you're able to speak. You're understanding me Liz, you're talking and making sense. Your speech is a little off, but that's to be expected. Your head took a hard hit. Doctors have been waiting for the swelling to reduce to determine the extent of your injuries. You're passing the test with flying colors."

"The pain in my head is, uh, enough to make a preacher cuss, Colleen. Remove the axe from my skull, then get me out of this bed."

"The pounding will have to go away on its own, give it a few days. You have to bear it until then, but I can make you more comfortable. Let me get a different pillow under your neck," she said, as she rolled it in place. "And this cool, damp cloth will feel good. I'll soften the lights. There," she said as the room grew dim.

"So, so that's why I can't remember anything?"

"Yup, that's why. Here, sip this," Colleen said, offering a tablet with a straw in a glass of water.

"Then can you remind me why my right side doesn't move? Why there is a bandage that starts on my left shoulder? I'm, uh, afraid to see where it ends. I'd lift the sheets to look for myself if I could, but my left arm feels like lead and my right is about as useful as a, a, a steering wheel on a mule. Nothing feels right, holy hell, I can't even lift the, uh, the damn sheets!"

"Your right side is paralyzed, Liz. It may be

temporary. To recover, your brain has to get well. But Doctor Jenkins thinks as the swelling goes down, you might regain the use of your arm and leg. It will take some therapy to get you back to full speed, but that's something we know how to do," she said.

"And the bandage? What giant hole is it covering up?"

"Liz, when the Japs slammed the hospital, your left side took a direct hit. Debris from the blast thumped your head. It also sheared off your left forearm. The doctors amputated below the elbow to save your life."

Liz shut down. "No, no," she whispered in a low and guttural growl. Tears rolled down her cheeks. "I can't be a cripple. I can't be an amputee. I'm uh, I'm a nurse. I need my arms, my legs. I can't work without them. NO! NO!" she begged. "Please, please Colleen, this just can't be true." She heaved a great and deep groan from somewhere within; a convulsive sob racked her chest. She couldn't wipe the runny nose and tears that ran down her soggy face.

Colleen pressed a tissue on her cheeks to clean the mess. "You're alive, Liz, you're alive. That's most important. First, we'll get you well. After that, we'll figure out what's next."

"I can't Colleen, I can't, I can't do this. I w-w-w-won't. I can't be a one-armed nurse, so what is the point? Don't ask this of me. I use my hands all day, every day. What good am I without them? Leave me alone. Let me die." A loud moan rose from her throat and wailed through the air.

"I will not. I'm going to get you feeling human once more," Colleen said, placing a brush on her hair, taking the first gentle stroke, "and get you out of here. Then we're going to move mountains, Nurse Kizer, to find Van."

Colleen did not know how to fulfill her promise, and Liz was inconsolable. But as the days passed, and her right side strengthened, the old, irrepressible Liz showed up on occasion and started to make progress.

"What can I do for you?" Colleen asked for the tenth day in a row, although she already knew and had initiated the routine.

Liz tried to smile and chat, a leap ahead of the dark days of denial, but Colleen missed the natural effervescence, the contagious optimism she used to bring to every conversation. Reversing roles, Colleen found herself playing cheerleader to Liz.

"Give me a minute to get everything in order," she said, "then I'll finish up with the world's greatest scalp massage, the best one ever. It's my specialty, my treat, free of charge. I'll fill you in on what you've missed, while I'm doing it."

"Bless you, dearie, it's a deal," Liz whispered. Her speech had shown steady improvement, and the stammers were mostly gone.

As she rolled over, she grimaced at the sharp, stabbing pains, constant reminders of her phantom arm. "Talk fast, take my mind off this.

Tell me everything." Her interest seemed real.

Colleen told Liz all that had happened since they last hugged goodbye, while massaging her carefully and deliberately to relax Liz's taut muscles and release her pent-up stress. She gently pressed her fingers on Liz's ragged hairline around the jagged stitches where she had sustained the blow.

When Liz whispered through drowsy speech, "I met a guy," Colleen didn't think she'd heard her correctly. She leaned in.

"What is it, Liz, what did you say?"

"A guy, his name is Corporal Jerry Palmer." She stared at the wall, recalling. It still taxed her strength to simultaneously think and talk and breathe.

"He saw Van, was with him on Guadalcanal. Thinks he was airlifted out but didn't know more than that."

"That's wonderful, Liz. It means Van's alive and being cared for somewhere by a wonderful nurse."

"I hope so. No word of him since, so I still don't know where he is, or how he is."

"He's alive, and we'll find him."

"Jerry was a dairy farmer from North Dakota before he joined the army, a really nice guy. Completely out of place in a foreign country. He reported for duty in Hawaii before he shipped out and joked that the islands were so stunning, living there for a couple of months almost made losing a leg a fair trade. Have to say, I disagree."

Colleen completed the massage, and Liz drifted off with deep breaths and a relaxed body. Mission accomplished. Her next mission would be to find Captain Van Kizer before Liz lost faith.

STORY

Chapter Nineteen

*You are remembered for
the rules you break.*

GENERAL DOUGLAS MACARTHUR

❊   ❊   ❊

Colleen returned to the barracks feeling optimistic and visited every day after to do what she could for her friend. She felt the reward on the third Sunday afternoon, when she found Liz sitting up in bed, wanting to eat, wanting to renew her strength. Colleen stood beside her, holding a fork to her mouth. When Liz finished, Colleen opened the sandwich from the mess she'd brought for herself and poured a cup of water from the carafe on the tray.

Following lunch, Colleen lifted Liz into a wheelchair and pushed her on a long walk around the base. She found a bench beneath a tree and parked the chair next to it. She locked it securely, then took a seat next to Liz. From the bag hanging on the back of the chair, Colleen took two cookies, holding one out to Liz and keeping one for herself. Rest and fresh air away from the hospital was good for them both.

The swelling in Liz's brain had reduced, and her speech had improved, but she had a long way to go before her body would allow her to function in any professional capacity. She had regained her vocabulary, although enunciation of certain letters remained poor. She still showed some deficits in comprehension and recall. Today's conversation would be good practice for her.

Liz had been unable to remember her experience completely and appeared to still be in shock, but flashbacks had been coming more often. Under the shade of a huge, old elm and a sky filled with clouds floating in a peacock blue pool, the story started to drift out. Breezes gently blew, birds sang in harmony and Liz began to find her voice again, leaning on the comfort of Colleen's shoulder.

"You really can't know what it's like unless you're there, Colleen," she said, slurring only a few syllables. "I was anxious every minute. Everything was crazy, out of control. But I've never been more challenged, or more inspired, as a nurse. Seeing what our guys are going through, getting to do my part, that was very gratifying. I will never forget it."

"We have to find a way for you to be a nurse

again, Liz. That's your job now, get well and find a new way. It's why I'm here. You can count on me to help you get there."

"I know, Colleen, I also know I'll never be the same." She spoke thoughtfully, deliberately. "Look at me. My body's broken, my brain barely clicks. I think about each word before I can say it. I can't remember big chunks of my life. I don't have enough vitality to get me through a day. I'm still uncertain about a lot that happened."

"You're healing, Liz. This is gonna' take a while. Be kind to yourself. Tell me what's going on in that head of yours. Let's sort it all out, like you always do with me."

"I'm not sure. Even before I was knocked unconscious, I was often confused about things going on there."

"What was your initial assignment?"

"Well, first they sent our flying ambulance to Horaniu. I flew several missions from there, then onto Vella Lavella, when the fighting heated up on the island.

"Often, it was hard to tell who the enemy was. The Japs were dropping bombs on our heads. The natives were bringing their babies to us, wanting us to fix their burned faces, reattach tiny arms or legs, repair a blind eye or a stomach bloated by starving, you name it. They lived on the land the Japs occupied, and our guys fought to claim. Our guys died taking it from them as part of the Allied strategy. Does that make them the enemy, too?

Was I supposed to hate them?"

"I don't know, Liz, if you're supposed to hate them, but it's a waste of your precious energy now. You have more important things to dwell on."

"They were so pleased by anything we did. To thank us, those parents brought sacks of fresh fruit they picked. What they offered us was the only decent thing we ate."

Colleen poured water from her canteen into a cup and held it up to Liz's mouth. "I'm so glad they fed you. I'm not sure you'd be here if they hadn't supplemented your diet."

"Agreed," Liz said, swallowing hard. "It was terrible. Everyone was hungry. We tried to forget our misery by singing Christmas carols. It was summer, not December, but we knew the words. They sang back to us. I don't know what they said, but it sounded mighty nice. In any case, it was the only sweet moment of the whole war."

"I read all about you in the Courier Journal."

"Oh, yeah?" Liz's expression changed from sad to surprised.

"You're famous. They printed a picture of you, too, along with the article. One copy is in the Bowman Field library. I saved another for your scrapbook." Colleen smiled remembering the pride she felt when she showed the article to Miss Vernon.

"Hmm, I didn't know. There was a journalist who embedded with us for a while. His name was Charles Dempsey. He made our base his headquarters. He'd roam the country in a jeep during the day and come back to stay with us at night. We'd eat dinner with him, and he'd tell us what he saw."

"The story he wrote about you is very flattering."

"There were so many interesting people, he could have written about any of them. Everyone I met was extraordinary in their commitment, in their tenacity. Once, a pipe burst during a flight, the plane filled with steam. I thought we were crashing for sure. So did everyone else from the looks on their faces, but no one panicked. The co-pilot jumped up, grabbed a few tools and saved the day. He fixed the pipe while the pilot evaded enemy fire on both sides by himself. We landed, no one a hero. All part of a day's work." She stared into the distance, recalling the scene.

"That sounds a little too close for comfort," Colleen said, patting her hands.

"Way too close. But when you're in the middle of it, your adrenaline takes over. You don't think about the danger. You think about the patients. I kicked into overdrive and forgot to worry until later, when I realized what we came through. I heard the pilots talking. They don't mince words."

"What was it like to serve in the field hospital?"

"Oh, you should have seen the set-up, Colleen," she said. For the first time, her face lit up. "It was basically a trailer house pretending to be an operating room, complete with tables, surgical instruments and x-ray equipment. We made do without clean, running water. The power blew if the wind blew, and the generator that supplied backup for lights and equipment often didn't work, leaving us in the dark mid-surgery with tools we couldn't use. When we ran out of blood, which happened frequently, we drained the bodies of staff and healthy soldiers on duty."

The wind had kicked up and Colleen wrapped a blanket around Liz's shoulders. "Sounds to me like you did what you had to do."

Liz shook her head in disbelief, thinking of the risks she had taken.

"Caring for patients under those conditions must have taxed everyone to the max."

"It did, but we made it work. You would be pleased. I sure was. Anywhere the trucks went, the mobile surgery went, so we were as close to the front as possible, operating under the most dangerous conditions on knees that shook, still saving lives."

"Very impressive," Colleen replied. She meant it.

Liz shifted her weight in the chair, trying to evade the bed sore that was developing on her bottom. "We did our best to avoid gunshots and capture as we followed the men around. During the land battles, our guys were fighting hand to hand with the Japs, which is like trying to win a knife fight in a phone booth. They fought to the death. We'd haul the guys off the field to the mobile as fast as possible to triage them---bleeding, crying, maggots eating their raw flesh and sucking their blood, losing life right in front of us. As soon as we filled the plane, we flew them out. A C-47 waiting in the tropical sun becomes an oven on the inside, so temperatures would be as high as one hundred and forty, one hundred and fifty degrees while we loaded and began the flight. We'd slam the door shut and swelter." She felt as if sweat was rolling down her back despite the cool breeze.

"Heat like that would do me in," Colleen said, imagining how difficult movement would be under those conditions.

"Then we froze once we increased altitude. But without quick intervention, those frightened, gravely wounded men would have died. We did this over and over. It seems impossible there is anybody left to fight."

"Sadly, there are new recruits on both sides."

"I saw that what we do makes a difference, Colleen. The guys I brought out wouldn't have lasted long enough to get to a hospital in an ambulance. If we hadn't loaded them on those planes and sent them out of there, well, I know we saved lives."

The clouds had begun to darken, and Colleen suspected rain was due. "I know you did too, Liz, because I met one of your fans. Do you remember Corporal Tyson Keaton?"

Liz strained to remember, then said, "Sure, I remember Tyson. You met him?"

"We treated him for a week before he headed back to San Diego. He wants to see you and thank you."

"He was a good guy. All of them were, but that group was special. We flew nineteen hours over jungle and ocean. I didn't know how big the world is."

"Corporal Keaton sings your praises."

"He should praise the crew. They were outstanding. The medical staff sergeant, the pilots, everybody pitched in to insure we got the guys out of there."

"Just know that you have a very grateful fan."

"Glad to hear. One of those talented Brits I met operated on Tyson. Several of their surgeons rotated through our operating rooms."

"What kind of surgeons were they?"

"The excellent kind, their work was superb. They didn't interfere with me. I took full charge of my patients. They stayed out of my way, unless I asked for help. They were a great example that when smart people have faith that they can do something, they succeed. They were bold; they were genius. It's funny, in the middle of a war zone, while napping on a bomb bag, I felt safe, beside them. They were that sure."

Colleen sensed a sort of peace settle over Liz. She appeared calm, serene.

"Was your Bowman training sufficient to the task?"

Liz thought for a moment before answering.

"Being on Vella Lavella is like being on another planet, not a good fit. But I knew enough to stay calm, and that gave me the assurance to think about how to solve the problem. Not much goes by the book in a war zone. I must have broken every rule at least once, but I learned how to keep myself alive, and those who depended on me. Thank you for that." She smiled at Colleen; it was heartfelt.

Colleen returned the warmth but said, "I feel guilty. You were injured and are paying a stiff price for your service. I pay nothing."

"Thank heavens, you don't. It serves no point. You didn't cause that blast to hit me in the head, Colleen. The Japs did. That had nothing to do with you. I wanted to be there, remember? I volunteered. We each have our job to do. That was mine, this is yours."

"It doesn't seem fair, or enough, next to your sacrifice."

"The front was tough. Maps weren't accurate and we got lost. Periods of constant rain nearly drowned us and made struggling up and down slippery hills and sharp reefs almost impossible. Clinging vines grew over everything, we used them to pull ourselves along. The streams we crossed became rivers by the time we returned. The men labored in hot and heavy gear that got soaked."

"That's terrible!"

"The jungle was a labyrinth of swamps covered by a dense overgrowth of exotic plants, so we could only see a few feet ahead, rendering the enemy invisible and causing widespread panic. The panic caused chaos. Our guys threw grenades blindly in the dark. Some of them hit trees, bounced back and exploded among us, injuring our own people."

"Oh, how awful!"

"It was, and that's just the beginning. Killer heat and humidity is a perfect environment to breed those mosquitos that left a trail of malarial breadcrumbs, but I also treated typhus and hepatitis, plus the occasional case of polio, plus every skin disease I've ever heard of---dermatitis, a fungus of the ear canal, athlete's foot that spreads to elbows and fingers. Then there were the worms---flatworms, roundworms, pinworms, whipworms, tapeworms and hookworms, all of which led to severe anemia, lethargy and headaches."

"Gosh! Deadly mosquitos and disgusting worms. How did you deal with that?"

"With lots of netting, sprays, long sleeves and pants, tucked in from head to toe, a very uncomfortable thing to do in that climate. They lived to suck our blood. But that's not the worst of it. It's so humid, that disposing of the dead ASAP is an important job. The bloated bodies rot very quickly, leading to huge swarms of breeding, feeding, disease spreading flies, along with the wickedest smells."

"Well, that's just gross."

"Indeed! So was the diarrhea that afflicted

everyone, and the chronic digestive problems from the invisible bacteria we swallowed with every drop of water, along with the inedible food from our mess kits."

"You don't ever get to complain about gaining an extra five again, you hear?"

"Don't worry. I've never been so glad to eat real food. I'll never take it for granted. Neither will our guys. On the plane, they struggled to eat. It was tough to feed them when they're strapped down and can't sit up."

"I believe it. What pressure!"

"Yes, but we managed. We could make do if there was some food on board, but that didn't happen often. Adjusting patient care while flying and getting drug treatments right in changing altitudes, none of it went smoothly. I mean, how can you be in ten places at once?"

"Good question."

"One I never could answer. Then, someone would puke and everyone would puke. The plane's ventilation system was inadequate. Odor in a closed space like that is atrocious."

"I can see you standing in a slippery aisle, ministering to your men as you slide by, trying hard not to breathe."

"That's not the worst of it, either. After the puking came bedpans and urinals. No one can move, most need help, so that was another interesting interlude in my busy flight. Guess where I emptied the bedpans on one of those trips?"

"Where?"

"Oh, forget I said it. It's too nasty to tell. Let's just say that's a memory I wish I could forget."

"OK, we'll let that one go."

"Just as bad were the thermoses with the seals that melted, letting all the water leak out. On one flight, I carried one thermos for all of us. When it was empty, I told them, 'That's all there is'. That flight seemed the longest, adding thirst on top of everything else. I learned how to talk baseball to take their minds off it."

"I bet that made you popular."

"Not at all. Everyone was dehydrated. The only things available to me were aspirin, bicarbonate of soda, iodine, Merthiolate and some peppermint tablets. The medical kits were always heavy and bulky, yet undersupplied. I didn't have any penicillin when I needed it. Nothing for psychotic patients. One of them, a violent one, grabbed a gun and threatened to shoot the pilot if we didn't turn around and pick up his buddy. Trouble is, his buddy was dead, and we only saved room for the living."

"What did you do?"

"We managed to overtake him and get the gun, but we had a long flight before us and he was out of his mind---screaming, banging his head. We restrained him with whatever we could find---a belt around his hands, ropes around his feet. When I came to feed him or check on him, he'd lash out however he could, biting, spitting, shouting obscenities."

"What happened to him?"

"Who knows? When I dropped him at the hospital, I gave instructions for psych care, but there was no place for him. Like the other thousand dogfaces I saw, I'll never know what happened to any of my guys. I just pray they made it."

"You know what happened to Tyson. He made it."

"During his flight, everyone was starving. No one had eaten. I cleaned up puke from air sickness, fed them the small amount of food that was available, then cleaned that up when they puked it out, too. Some were cold. There were never enough blankets."

"Tyson said he never saw you eat."

"Oh, there was not enough for me, and everything happened too fast. Everyone needed everything. After they were delivered to the hospital, then I ate."

"Do you remember what happened when you were hit?"

"Not much. I was attending Dr. Jax. We were removing shrapnel from a private's abdomen. Next thing I know, I'm on a plane to Walter Reed in DC. What a relief. My brain was so scrambled by then I didn't know what was going on, except that something was terribly wrong."

"I was with Chantel at the Red Cross when I

found out you were coming here. You can imagine my surprise. I was thrilled to know we'd be together but concerned by the description of your injuries. Thank heavens they sent you to Nichols, so I can help."

"Can't think of anyone I'd rather have nagging me. Sorry for writing only one letter to you. I meant to do better. Don't think I forgot about you. It's just that the only place quiet enough to write was that trench. I didn't enjoy being there that much."

"Hey, it's ok. You were a little busy. So was I. What matters is, you're here now."

Although it had taken three full weeks before Liz could have that conversation, seeing her alert and engaging was extremely encouraging. The language center of her brain was recovering. *Perhaps as healing continues, she'll regain full control over her right side. Maybe her muscles will strengthen sufficiently. Maybe she'll be able to move better and speak more clearly.*

Colleen unwrapped a piece of hard candy and dropped it on Liz's tongue, then unwrapped a second for herself. She popped it on her tongue and said, "Tell me, my friend, is there more you'd like to say about what happened to you?"

"You won't believe me if I do," Liz said, "and I don't have the words to describe it. I mean, what does complete fear look like? Or being so hungry you'll eat just about anything. Golly, I've never experienced such pain before, the way my stomach hurt, my whole insides, when we didn't have adequate food."

"How were you able to survive it, Liz? How did you do it?"

"I honestly don't know. My guardian angel? Bullets whizzed past my head. Shrapnel flew in every direction. Some of the guys were on the ground delirious with fever, weak from dysentery. While I'm treating them, others were shot and fell beside me, their faces in the dirt."

"It must have been terrifying."

"Yes, and all I wanted to do was help people. When I couldn't, it overwhelmed me. It exhilarated me, too. You've never seen such bravery, so many people trying so hard in preposterous circumstances, scared to death, trying to do the right thing. The guys can't fathom why their pal is killed, or why their leg is in a ditch somewhere, just so the Allies can say we took this rock. They struggled with that, so did I. But even though I didn't always grasp what was going on, I have never been more connected, more committed to a cause. Plus, I saw the most astonishing surgeries and practiced the most fascinating medicine. Wow! What those docs can do!"

"Ooooh. I'm jealous. Tell me more."

"You have to know the situation to fully appreciate what they did. I saw it for myself, between flights, at the mobile hospital. We were less than twenty minutes from the fighting, close enough to facilitate rescue, far enough out of the way so we were not targets and our guys didn't have to take unnecessary risks to protect us. The war was swinging back and forth, we were swinging with it. We were shocked by how badly wounded the men were. God, Colleen, their bodies were destroyed, parts blown off, blood pumping out like through a sieve, burns so bad. No one should have to bear what they do. The thing that amazed me was how they acted when they were lined up outside the operating rooms with their miserable, broken bodies. Not once did I hear anyone complain."

"I treated a patient at Nichols last Sunday who griped about a throat swab."

Liz laughed, which she had rarely done since her return. It was so good to see her beautiful smile once more.

"I teamed up with sixteen other nurses from all over---England, Australia, Canada. Those gals were terrific. We lived together under the same tarp, just like the guys at the front. I thought I was tough, but they could really take it."

"Proving nurses are fabulous everywhere," Colleen said, feeling enormous pride in her profession.

"Remember how thrilled we were with our boots when we received our new uniforms at graduation? Clearly, they are not recommended for the tropics. They were useless for walking the terrain, so heavy and slick and inflexible. They gave us blisters on our very hot feet. Even our underwear rotted. I wore men's boxers 'cause that's all Uncle Sam could find for the ladies to use for replacements. My prized coveralls are in tatters, too."

"I know, I saw them. I think Uncle Sam owes you a new uniform. I'm pretty sure he's got an extra in your size if you ask nicely."

"My feet would benefit from some TLC. Can I just wear slippers forever?"

"As long as you like, dear one. Your feet deserve the best. They are a disaster."

"Thanks for the bedside manner, Nurse O'Brien. Do you flatter all your patients that way?"

"No, I apologize, but I surveyed the damage earlier. Let's take a look, shall we?" she asked, removing Liz's socks. "How did that happen?"

Together they examined the boils, abscesses, blisters, cuts, bruises and bumps that turned her petite, formerly polished toes into something akin to a boxer's face after the twelfth round. They'd had the hell beaten out of them.

"The rains were a real frog wash, so my boots would get wet, or my feet would sweat, then swell. Then the boots would get tight and rub blisters everywhere, including some places I never knew existed---between my toes, under toenails that hadn't been trimmed in months. It hurt when they dug into my flesh."

"I noticed. Your toes are full of pus, which is why I'm going to give you a treatment, then a pedicure. I brought my bag. Let me lift your right leg into my lap, and I'll get to work."

Colleen placed Liz's foot between her knees and set out her tools. Liz leaned back and also noticed the dark clouds forming overhead. "Now, relax and savor the next hour on this magnificent Kentucky day. I'll pamper your feet in our outdoor spa under this gorgeous tree," Colleen said, selecting the clippers, "and we'll get it done before the storm."

"It's so peaceful to rest in a place of such splendor. There was no rest in the Solomons. The emergencies during battle swamped us. Everyone worked regular hours, plus all the extras, without counting them, then got ready for the next round. We couldn't keep up. The current crop of boys had to leave to make room for the next wave. We'd get 'em in, fix 'em up and move 'em out. I could never give my feet a break. And if I didn't put my boots on, well, that's why there are bruises and cuts."

"I'm so sorry you walked all those hours on aching feet."

"Me, too, except what I saw in my patients was so much worse than anything that happened to me."

"Let me make it up to you a bit by lathering you with lotion," Colleen said, after wiping them with a sterile rag and dabbing medicine on the sores. "When your skin is soft, I'll trim the cuticles, clean out the pus and finish with two coats of Mrs. Miniver polish, your favorite."

"Oh, thank you, darlin'. You have no idea how

much this helps. Your kind touch soothes my soul. It just might have the power to make me feel good again."

"Glad to do it, Liz. Hold still, I'm going to pumice the calluses with this stone."

"Good riddance. They're hard as a rock. I felt them every step I took."

"You are at Bowman now, clean, fed, rested and cared for. I know hospital food is not the best, but it's better than field rations. You must eat more of it, Liz. We've got to get you strong, back to full energy, so you can walk out of here on your own two feet."

"I'm trying, but my appetite got lost in that jungle, along with everything else. It's hard to force food down, even when it's essential to do so. I don't think I will walk out of here. I'm tired of pretending everything is going to be ok. My right arm's bending and moving better and better, but not my leg. It's about as useful to me as a screen door on a submarine. The exercises are a big waste of effort."

"You possess many gifts, Liz, except for the gift of patience. Use it or lose it, my friend. You can't quit, you have to find the will to use it. To persevere. The therapy is rebuilding your muscles, retraining your nervous system, helping with balance and stabilizing your core. Keep working at it every day. You'll get there."

"I'm not impatient, I'm realistic. I see the damage done, understand the prognosis and the progress I've made. It's not in the cards for me to sprint down the aisle of an airplane."

"We don't know what's possible yet, so we'll keep trying. We can't give up. We'll do everything we can to get you to the other side of this," Colleen said, handing Liz a Kleenex tissue to dry the tears that began, finally, to fall. "Let it out, Liz, it's ok," she said softly, taking her hand.

"I missed the darndest things over there," Liz said, forcing a smile after a long sob. She dabbed her eyes. "I would have given anything for a box of these and a decent fountain pen," she said. "Come to think of it, I missed the Devil, too. What's been going on there?"

"Haven't been since our last trip."

"What? That's a real shame. You were supposed to keep my seat warm, so it's still waiting for me."

"It's always waiting for you. When you're ready, I'll take you."

"Is that a promise?"

"I promise you, Elizabeth Kizer, if you'll eat and co-operate with the therapist on your exercises, I will personally take you to the Air Devils Inn and buy whatever you like for dinner."

"I've been eating K-rations. A hamburger at the Devil will taste like fine dining in the Oak Room by comparison."

"Uh, no burgers, no meat. How about a steaming baked potato, loaded with anything but butter and cheese?"

"Ugh, no thanks, rain check. I could use some fun, though. There was no social life in that godforsaken place. I haven't seen a paved road, a town or a dress shop, let alone a party. We worked, slept and wrote a few letters, that's it, all while terrified."

"Please don't put that on the recruiting poster. We're still hiring more nurses, until this bloody mess is called off by someone who loves peace."

She glanced at the sky. "Look at those clouds, Liz. They're getting darker and the wind is starting to whip. I think we may be minutes away from a downpour. I better get you back to your room," Colleen said, putting her supplies back into her bag and hanging it on the back of the wheelchair.

She unlocked the chair and started the long walk back to the hospital. "When this is over, we are going to return to the good life, you and me, where you can party all night long if you want to."

"We'll shop for something pretty to wear if I still remember how. You forget about money when there is no place to spend it. There wasn't anything to buy on the island, so every penny of my one hundred and eighty-six dollars per month got split with Ma. The other half waits for me in my bank account."

"My bank account's looking better, too. I've saved every nickel I could. I think I'll have enough when my tour is up to make a down payment on a little home for me and Chloe."

"How is your little doll baby? She must be

talking well by now."

"Mama says she sings *Old MacDonald*, recites some nursery rhymes and is learning her alphabet. Mama says she's whip smart, but I knew that."

"You must be so anxious to see her. It won't be too long."

"Maybe sooner than later. Mama wrote that my cousin, Sean, talked to Tommy at Flanagan's. He's unemployed, so he received a notice to check in with the draft board."

"What about Grandma O'Brien? Will she get in a duel with your Mama to take Chloe from her?"

Colleen scanned the sky as thunder roared in the distance and lightening flashed in the east. She pushed the chair around the corner and continued down the final stretch of the path, walking at a rapid pace. "Nah, not likely. She's still raising the last three from her brood of nine. I don't think she's eager to take on her grands. If she is, others need her more than Chloe. Her daughter's twins have been neglected since birth. Both parents are alcoholics, a really distressing situation. And Tommy knows Mama's got the pictures of my bruises, that she's likely to show them to Father O'Malley if he causes me more trouble. She thinks that will help keep him in check. Tommy's a proud man. He's embarrassed, doesn't want anyone to know he lost his temper, doesn't want anyone to know he punched me."

"It's funny," said Liz, "as much as I tried to run away from home, all I could think about was my family. The other nurses talked constantly of theirs, too. I sure did miss mine. But none of us would have gone home, if given the chance. We were proud to be nurses, proud to be with our guys. I'd still be there if I had worn my dang helmet on my head."

"Not sure your helmet would have saved your noodle from a hit like that, but the extra protection from sturdy steel certainly would have helped."

"I used that thing for every purpose but the one it was intended for. It turned out to be my most valuable tool. I cooked in it, sat on it, used it to carry water from the stream to bathe in."

"Too bad you didn't use it as a helmet. Maybe you should ask for two of them next time."

"At least I'm caught up on my rest. A bed feels luxurious after months of using my duffle for a mattress and a parachute for a pillow. We used tarp as walls for a bit of privacy, but when we slept, it sounded like a room of buzzsaws."

"That must have been ugly."

"Oh, we were ugly for sure. Mud and sweat were constant. The heat and humidity grew mold on any surface. Nothing stays clean in that environment. Our showers hinged on rainwater, which we collected and poured on our heads. We had no bath soap, nothing to clean ourselves with, no shampoo, no creams, no laundry flakes."

"So, everyone was dirty all the time?"

"Yep, we were. We did laundry by hand. Our clothes were stiff and smelly. Some of the guys invented an ingenious washing machine for us out of oil drums driven by the wind, but mostly we used the river and a rock."

"Wait until you see the new Bendix in the women's barracks. It's completely push button and simple to use."

"That is good to have, almost as good as a flushing toilet. The latrine was primitive, to say the least. Oh! The flies! The stench from the toilet drove you out as quickly as you could move, not to mention the lizards, spiders and other creeping things, who observed and commented by making their own squeaky noises. Eventually, we just peed on the ground since urine is sterile and frequent rains washed it away."

"There is that saving grace."

"Then we ran out of all things female, so we improvised during our monthlies. That was interesting. Please, never ever."

"Just like in the good old days."

"The bad old days for sure."

"If you feel up to it, we'll get you in the shower tomorrow. No more spit baths for you."

"You have no idea how excited I am to have clean, warm water falling on my head, how eager I am to sit on a proper toilet and indulge in the right amount of effort for a quality pee and poo. Get me on my feet so I can dismiss the bedpan aide forever."

"OK, great, we have two goals to point towards. We'll dedicate every moment to getting you in the shower and on the potty. Lofty aspirations to start the week."

They had arrived at the front door. Colleen pushed her through it and down the hall to her room, just as the storm came crashing outside. As she lifted her friend into bed, Liz said, "Nurses are used to seeing plenty of misery, and I did. Despite the ugliness, though, almost every day I saw authentic acts of courage. I held the hands of men dying bravely and received the blessing of sharing that moment with them. I heard the voices of freedom through the army radio and witnessed the most spectacular sunrises. Each morning I'd get up and think, maybe if the earth can awake fresh and alive each day, I can, too. That kept me going."

"That sounds like the Liz I know and love. Let's get you back out there, girlfriend, to look for the sunrise every morning."

"The army is sending me on indefinite leave after I get out of here. They say I deserve R and R, but I think they don't believe it's possible for me to run with the big dogs. They want me to stay behind and sit on the porch."

"That's your opinion. It's not a fact. They're talking about you taking a break, not about sitting on the porch. You've never had a vacation, have you?"

"No, what will I do with myself?"

"Whatever you want. Take advantage of this opportunity on Uncle Sam's dime. He wants you to take care of yourself first, then climb off the porch. That's all. It's mighty nice of Sam to offer that time to you."

"I'm not familiar with free time, I won't know how to use it."

"You will learn."

"I'll try, but all I know for sure is, I want to go back."

DIVERSION

Chapter Twenty

The only thing you have
to fear is fear itself.

PRESIDENT FRANKLIN D. ROOSEVELT

❊ ❊ ❊

Colleen had Labor Day off work and spent a rare two hours sunning with a few other nurses at a swimming party at the YWCA, thanks to the benevolence of the ladies of the USO. These formidable women sold war bonds like professionals, lived by the motto "waste not, want not" and recycled everything for the good of the war effort. Colleen watched them refill well-worn empty cardboard boxes with matches rather than ask for new.

After the party, she returned to the base to spend the rest of the holiday with her peers. To conserve gas and rubber, no one had organized a parade like in the past, but they did arrange for a Goddess of Liberty tableau. Some of the men pitched horseshoes, adding the clinking sounds of steel wrapping around pegs to the general cacophony of laughter and the shouts of the players, both winners and losers. A performance by the drum and bugle corps, plus air exhibition drills of all kinds, were always impressive to see, but Colleen had already witnessed them on several occasions. She wanted something else.

She walked into hangar one, where enough potato salad to feed an army, plenty of hot dogs and sheet cakes galore meant everyone ate all they wanted. No picnic ever tasted as good as this one, served on a day of cool breezes and a quick, cleansing shower, followed by a golden sun shedding light on foliage preparing the breathtaking burnt oranges and ruby reds of fall.

Later in the evening, the show at the armory cost Colleen and her friends twenty cents each. The entertainment, hosted by Miss Kentucky and her court, was well worth it.

But it was the sing-along around the piano player at Casey's Bar and Grill, where the women stopped for a snack on the way home, that turned out to be the most fun on this near-perfect day. They joined those standing behind Mac, whose black hands tapped forcefully and gracefully on the white keys of the upright Baldwin. Dark sunglasses, back straight, head held high, totally immersed in the rapture of the music emanating from his fingertips, Mac's bliss was contagious.

He brought the whole room to life. Everyone swayed, swooned and tapped to the harmonies he produced, coasting from one melody to another, all from memory.

With just one glass of wine, Colleen could lose her inhibitions enough to belt out with the rest of them the songs she remembered. A mix of people joined in, including a group of female mechanics who ran the sheet metal shop housed in the small building behind the hangar. They kept the vehicles and aircraft at Bowman in tiptop shape, proving they could perform maintenance as well as the guys. A few of the female air traffic controllers also sang along. These women watched Bowman's skies from the Crow's Nest and spoke with clear, firm voices when guiding planes to their landings. They were especially adept at their task because of their unflappability and attention to details. Tonight though, they cut loose and bellowed!

Some tunes brought a lump in Colleen's throat because of the memories they evoked. *We danced to Only Forever at our wedding. I remember how much I wanted Tommy to hold me in his arms, forever,* she recalled. She closed her eyes and pictured the scene; their families gathered in the church hall, music playing, lights glowing, Tommy slowly guiding her around the floor while her simple gown, sewn by Gran, twirled around her. He held her close enough she could smell him and sense his masculinity. The sensation of it caused her to hold tightly to him, anticipating the moment they would finally be alone.

Another tune jolted her, *Over the Rainbow*. *That one always sends chills up my spine,* she thought. *Tommy and I used to sing it in high school chorus. His deep baritone drowned out everyone else.*

Sister Mary Mark, in her second year as a nun and first year on the faculty of St. Patrick's School, had livened up the music curriculum quite a lot. Students hung out in the chorus room after school with the rest of their friends and rehearsed for a performance. It became a popular activity, because Sister saved them from the dusty hymns they sang at Mass. Instead, she introduced them to a whole range of lively and interesting contemporary music, especially show tunes.

When both Father O'Malley, senior pastor at St. Pat's, and Sister Josephine, the principal, admonished her to be more circumspect, the parents objected. They appreciated Sister Mark's interest in their children and her ability to reach them. They implored Father to allow her to continue. She did, and the kids showed up in droves, if they weren't gleaning the fields during harvest or taking care of siblings on any day of the year.

When the spring program commanded both a standing ovation and two encores, Sister Mary Mark and her "Irish Singers" gained enough support to warrant the inclusion of a small sum in the school budget set out as a line item dedicated to sheet music.

The vision of Sister's exuberance had stuck with Colleen, offering inspiration. The discipline of learning her parts and committing them to memory, cooperating with the whole chorus to achieve the right blend of sounds and the fabulous feelings that form when singing lyrical music in a group had impacted her ever since. Those very habits had propelled her through the tough days of study during nursing school. The pleasure she derives from singing was the best therapy for getting through tough days now.

Her favorite memories of Tommy came from the nights they stayed home, sitting around the fire in winter, or on the porch in summer, often with friends and family, talking through the day's events. The men pounded their beers on the table after telling the most outrageous tales. Before long, someone would start singing. Another would riff on the harmonica or strum a banjo or guitar, becoming the spark for a spontaneous hootenanny.

During those days, Tommy sang through their repertoire, blending his voice with her lilting soprano. Chloe rocked to the melody wearing a look of delight and amazement on her sweet face. In those moments, Colleen counted her blessings, every single one, and placed them carefully into her heart brimming with desire. How did all that degenerate into everything she both feared and despised?

"Tommy thought it too hokey, but *Over the*

Rainbow was my theme song," Colleen said to the nurse standing closest, Rita from Albuquerque. "I sang it to Chloe when we cuddled. It never occurred to me that sappy song would be relevant for my future, but humming it gets me going in the morning. Call me sentimental, but it moves me whenever I hear it."

"*White Christmas* does it for me. Isn't it enough to make you pray for snow? In the desert?" asked Rita.

"Not me. That's what we were singing at the factory holiday dinner when Tommy fell over, drunk, and created a scene. He embarrassed me so, I'll never forget that one."

Rita gave her a sympathetic, and knowing, squeeze of her hand.

"But the funny one I liked to sing to Chloe is *Elmer's Tune*, repeating the verses over and over while rocking her to sleep. She'd be out soon enough. I'd do my best to ease her into the crib. The second I'd stop singing, though, she'd wake up and want more, and we'd start the whole routine all over. I was so tired at times, I'd sing that song while I slept standing on my feet, one hand on Chloe's chest to settle her, the other on the wall to hold me up."

"You really miss your babe, don't you? I can see it in your face when you talk about her."

"I sure do," Colleen said, lifting one hand, "counting the months until I see her again." She dreamed about her homecoming that night, Chloe resting in her arms and receiving her precious kisses.

The next morning, Colleen was eager to chat with Liz, who usually liked to listen during a gossipy update. But that day she was listless, disinterested, unwilling to engage. After several futile attempts to connect, Colleen checked the chart. It was apparent her convalescence had plateaued. She no longer showed steady improvement. IVs and feeding tubes had been discontinued, she ate food by mouth and met every day with her therapists, but rather than grow stronger, her primary indicators turned downward. Nothing Colleen or the medical team did made a difference. Perhaps only one thing would.

Colleen went to see her friend, Corporal Richard Byers, whose desk sat in the office next to Captain Dorsey's. He'd helped her before, when he processed the papers authorizing her unusual appointment, and, more recently, when there was a snafu with her benefits. It still thrilled her to know that she earned some, the first for any employment she'd had.

"Hey, Corporal Byers, have a minute?" she asked, stepping in through the open door.

"I have an eternity for you, Nurse O'Brien," he said in his usual flirty manner. "Your wish is my command. What can I do for you?"

"My friend, Second Lieutenant Liz Kizer, is an

air evac nurse, except now she's in Nichols and not getting any better. She's giving up. Nothing I say or do motivates her to try. The only person who might is Captain Van Kizer, her husband. He went missing in action at Guadalcanal, but she heard from a Corporal Palmer that he was airlifted out. That's the last she knows of him. Are there any strings you can pull to find Captain Kizer?"

"Well, maybe, Colleen. I'll poke around and see what I can find out."

"Thank-you, Corporal. I'm really at my wit's end. Please try to locate the captain so he can help Liz get motivated again."

When more than two weeks passed without word from Corporal Byers, Colleen guessed that he had not been successful. *So glad I didn't mention that wild goose chase to Liz and raise her expectations. She could not take another disappointment.*

Three days later at Sunday lunch, Corporal Byers found her in the dining hall and handed her a slip of paper. "Last known whereabouts of Captain Van Kizer was Valley Forge General in Phoenixville, PA. He's not still there, but they have a record of where he went. Originally, he was hospitalized in critical condition, according to a doctor I spoke to, but he got out of the woods at Valley Forge. Doc says he'd been confined by his injuries until a few days ago, when they sent him to their rehab center. I got ahold of them today to confirm."

"Oh, Corporal Byers, you're a genius!"

"I know. There's more. Nurse Fay Guess will hold the phone to his ear this afternoon at 1400. Would Second Lieutenant Kizer like to speak to her husband?"

"Oh, yes, I'm certain she would. That's just the medicine she needs to get her out of that bed. I'll get Liz there, pronto."

"I'm a real whizz at dialing my rotary phone. We'll take the old girl out for a spin as soon as you bring Liz in."

"Thank you, thank you. You have done the impossible."

"Not impossible, Nurse O'Brien. I'll make sure it happens. Get the Lieutenant out of bed. It's afternoon in P. A."

"I owe you one, Corporal Byers."

"Nah, you're already giving all ya' got. Anything I can do for you, I will."

Colleen ran from the cafeteria and burst in on Liz, who was struggling mightily to put her right arm in the sleeve of her clean pjs.

"Get up, girlfriend, put your bonnet on. We're going for a ride."

"I don't have a bonnet and don't want a ride. I have absolutely nothing to rush to unless you count endless repetitions of leg lifts and arm stretches."

"You are in Louisville, Liz, where every woman has a bonnet, and you have a very big date in a very few minutes."

"Sure, I do. And did you hear I just won the Miss America pageant?"

"Corporal Byers, Dorsey's assistant, has found Van. He's recovering at Valley Forge in their rehab center. Byers thinks he can have you talking to him within the hour. Hurry up, let's go. He's waiting for us in his office."

"You found Van? Oh, my God, oh my God, get me dressed and out of this bed right now. Let's go! Let's go!"

Colleen helped Liz finish dressing and transitioned her to the chair. She was too eager to leave to bother with final touches. Her loose hair, without a barrette to hold it in place, flew about her face during the quick ride over.

Corporal Byers held the door and arranged a space for Liz to sit. He turned the dial on the phone. A crackling sound filled the room. They gathered near with ears pressed close. The hearing in Liz's left showed no improvement, but her right seemed good as new. She leaned in to listen from that side with the phone tucked between her shoulder and cheek.

After four long minutes of the Corporal's chatter, they heard a voice carried through the wires. "Hello? Hello?" it said, bounding clearly and calmly through the static.

"Van, Van is that you?" Liz screamed. A fraught pause later, Van could be heard calling out to her, "My lovely Lizzy, I've been wondering where in the hell you are."

"I'm here, in Louisville, KY at Nichols General. I've been looking everywhere for you. I can't believe I found you. I've missed you so much, darling. How are you, Van?"

Colleen gazed at the floor, embarrassed for intruding on this intimate moment, and walked into the hallway. Corporal Byers followed close behind.

"Doing better, thanks to the fine folks here," Van said. "They say I can leave in a few weeks, as long as I agree to further rehab at Camp Atterbury. But what are you doing at Nichols? When did you start working there?"

"It's a long story, darling, there is so much you don't know, so much I have to tell you."

"I'm all ears, Lizzy-Lou, got all day. What have you got to say? Tell me, please."

"Well, ok, to start with, I trained to be an air evac nurse so I could find you, then got a little banged up while on duty. That's why they sent me to Nichols."

"Exactly what does 'a little banged up' mean?"

"Let's just say for now that I've got to stay here a little longer, then I get some R and R. I'll ask them to send me to Atterbury. We can get through rehab together."

"The thought of that makes me so happy, Liz, you have no idea. I simply cannot wait to see you. How much longer...."

Static on the line abruptly ended the conversation. "Hey, sorry about that," Corporal

Byers said, coming in to take the phone. He began to redial, but the phone was dead. "This happens occasionally. It'll be down for a while, most likely. But it's ok to come back whenever you want after office hours. I'll hook you up, if you let me know you're on your way. Here's Captain Kizer's phone number and address, just in case you want to write a letter."

"You can count on it," Liz said, taking the note from him. "Is tomorrow too soon?"

Knowing Van was alive, that she could talk to him, would see him when her recovery allowed, provided the incentive Liz needed to recommit to her therapy. Colleen saw the difference immediately in their goofy banter as they returned to her room. Liz could not shut up. She could not wait to get started. Fear of the future would no longer stop her progress.

RESILIENCE

Chapter Twenty-One

With Freedom comes responsibility.

ELEANOR ROOSEVELT

❋ ❋ ❋

The last day Colleen spent with Liz was the same day Liz received the Distinguished Flying Cross. At 0900, Commander Jolson held the ceremony by the flagpole on the lawn in front of the headquarters. A full assemblage of officers and troops, plus all off-duty hospital personnel, stood at attention. He walked to the center of a stage lined with more flags, plus tall green palm fronds quickly but artfully arranged by USO volunteers. The band played the final verse of "God Bless America".

Colleen stood behind the chair holding her friend and realized the magnitude of the occasion. Liz sat refreshed in her new blues and crisp bow tie, her wings polished and shining, shoes waxed by Colleen the night before and stocking seams made straight within the last fifteen minutes, after a difficult struggle to pull them up a lifeless leg. Her overseas cap, tilted just so as only Liz could do, sat at a perky angle on hair brushed to burnished smoothness, except for one curly sprig popping out uninvited under the brim.

She was ready.

Colleen pushed Liz's chair onto the stage facing Commander Jolson. Liz nodded her head in salute; the music stopped. Everyone looked alert.

He cleared his throat to speak. "The well-trained American officer, who grasps her orders and works cooperatively to accomplish them, commits herself fully to everything she does. Second Lieutenant Elizbeth Abigail Kizer is one such officer. She is a true patriot."

Everyone turned toward Liz, causing a warm, pink blush to glow on her cheeks.

"During intense fighting in the South Pacific, their evac plane ran low on fuel. The pilot made a forced landing in the water near a small island. She, along with the crew, evacuated twenty-four patients stacked three-deep aboard a C-47.

"While landing, a propeller tore through the fuselage and severed the trachea of a patient. Lieutenant Kizer took various items she found, including an inflation tube from a life jacket, and made a suction tube. With this apparatus, she kept the man's airway open until aid arrived nineteen hours later. Her patient survived.

"Lieutenant Kizer, impaired by a sprained ankle and a back injury, insisted on attending to her patients and helped to load them onto life rafts as the plane sank. For these brave actions taken under great duress, for her uncompromising commitment to patients and crew, for her unflinching service to the United States of America, I promote Second Lieutenant Elizbeth Abigail Kizer to the rank of First Lieutenant and award her the Distinguished Flying Cross." He bent to pin the Cross on her uniform.

"She is an exemplary 'Lady with the Lamp'. She sets the very skies ablaze with promise for the sick and wounded, who are her sacred charges. She lives true to the Flight Nurse's Creed, 'I will not falter in war or in peace.' It must be said that the First Lieutenant did not falter in war. She will not falter in peace. Godspeed, First Lieutenant Elizabeth Kizer," he said, then saluted her. She was able to lift her right arm only part way to return it.

"I'm as full as a tick on a pig and ready to finish packing for Camp Atterbury," Liz said. "The sooner I get there, the sooner I see Van. Push me home, please?" she asked of Colleen. The long receiving line had dwindled, which included multiple pats-on-the-handshakes, personal congratulations, salutes, press photos, interviews and a generous serving of pink lemonade and white cake with green frosting despite a sugar and butter shortage.

"I cannot believe, Elizabeth Kizer, throughout

all these days together, during all of our talks, you did not bother to mention, not once, that you are a true hero," Colleen scolded, pushing Liz toward Nichols a little after noon. "When Chantel told me to get you here in full dress uniform, I didn't know this was the reason why. What gives?"

"What's to talk about? I did what was necessary. Nurses have knelt in blood on American battlefields since the Revolutionary War. It's not news."

"Yeah, don't be so modest, Liz. You nursed a patient with a sudden, violent and life-threatening injury, with no supplies and no plan, on a plane that's crashing. Yet somehow, despite your own injuries, you cobbled together a means to save that man's life, get the rest to dry ground and tend them until rescue. You're right, my mistake, it's no big deal."

"It wasn't, and I didn't do it alone. The crew worked with me and did things just as significant. Besides, I remember that flight differently, before we went down. One poor guy, Sergeant Lansing, endured a frightful compound fracture of his elbow joint. His whole arm was stiff and swollen, full of gangrene. To change the dressing, I moved it and could hear the bones crunching and grating inside. The guy turned his head away and never made a sound, just gritted his teeth, but I know it hurt like hell.

"I used scissors to carefully cut the gauze away, but the yards of packing were dried stiff and hard to pull off. A piece of it stuck to the splintered bone. He let out a sharp scream and a sob. The nerve endings were exposed and bare. I had to touch them with my forceps to remove the bandage. He was in agony and turned his head back toward me. I'll never forget the look in his eyes, his pupils clouded by pain. I almost quit. Not a word came out of him. No complaints. Just silence.

"I kept saying, 'I'm so sorry, I don't want to hurt you, but we must treat this infection to save your life.' Finally, he said, 'It's alright, nurse, carry on.' I saw his jaw clench, his hands curl into fists. He chewed the inside of his mouth bloody to distract from the thunderbolts shooting up his arm. I cleaned the wound, reset the splint. There were twenty-three other frightened and gravely wounded men on their way to dying aboard a crashing plane. I could not give Sargent Lansing the care his injuries demanded."

"What you described is even more admirable than what the Commander said, Liz. I don't know any nurse, including me, who could have done better under those conditions. You really are a hero."

"I don't feel like one, but I'm sure there are some. Everyone's survival depends on their adaptability, their cleverness, their resilience in a crisis. During that never-ending night, as the hours went on, it became harder to think. My hands moved automatically to stop the bleeding where possible. The swooning sounds of men fainting punctured the darkness. Every single man needed me. My hurried hands hurt Sargent Lansing. I haven't been able to shake the shame of it since. So, please, don't call me a hero."

Colleen opened the hospital door and pushed Liz down the hall to her room, pausing for the congratulations called out by staff and other patients along the way.

"You did something incredible under incredible circumstances, Liz," she said to her, parking the chair by the bed. "Give yourself a pat on the back. The United States military thinks you deserve it. The Commander awarded you the wings to prove it."

"I'm flattered, really, I am, I do appreciate the honor. I realize what it means. It's just I'd rather be flying on wings than wearing them."

"You'll figure out a way, Liz, if anyone can, to do the work you're meant to do. Finish your healing, give your love to Van, then decide what's next. When you do, when you leave Camp Atterbury, promise me you'll let me know where you and Van end up."

"You'll be the first to hear all about our reunion. I can never thank you enough for finding him for me, Colleen. How can I repay you?"

"I didn't find him, Corporal Byers did, and you don't owe us. Please, take care of yourself, Liz. We'll miss you. I'll miss you."

"I've got to get back to this war, Colleen. How can I go home to civilian life and that routine when

I know what's going on, when I felt most alive nursing in a war zone? Look at me. What good am I to them now? How can I help when I can barely help myself? I don't have much to offer anyone, do I?"

Just then the door opened and a tall man wearing a captain's uniform and a neat, dark mustache limped into the room, leaning on the hook of a cane. Clean, white gauze covered his most severe injuries. "You have a lot to offer me, Lizzie-Lou," he said, "and you can start by offering me a kiss." Liz spun around in her chair and let out a scream, "Van! My darling, Van. You're here! How? How did you get here? How did you find me? Oh, I don't care," she cried as she used her frail left foot to roll in clumsy lurches towards him.

He started to laugh and leaned in to embrace her, taking a moment to examine her face, now quivering with emotion. "Hi, lovely," he said, "you didn't think you could have a shindig like this and forget to invite me, did you?"

"No, of course, darling, I'm glad you're here, but how did you manage it?"

"Corporal Byers got wind of the Commander's plans and called me. Since I was ready to leave for R&R, the Corporal changed my travel dates. My car arrived late. I didn't want to interrupt the presentation and create a fuss, so I stayed behind the scenes. I heard every word Commander Jolson said though, Lizzie. I sure am proud of you. So, can you please show you're just as happy to see me by kissin' me right here, 'cause I sure am ready for ya' and don't think I can wait another minute."

With that he leaned awkwardly, but fully, into her, and she received him in return, laughing, crying, smelling him and rubbing his flesh to confirm his presence.

"I am so ready for you, too. I'll never let go," she said, nuzzling his neck.

Colleen began backing out the door. "You two have a lot to catch up. I'll get out of your way."

"Forgive me, Colleen. Van, this is Nurse Colleen O'Brien, my right and left arm. She's special, Van. She got me through evac training."

"Oh, hey, Nurse O'Brien," Van said, looking up. "Any friend of Liz is a friend of mine. I'd like to get to know you. Can we buy you something to drink, if that's alright with Liz."

Liz nodded, reenergized at the sight of her beloved. "Won't you join us for a beer at the Devils?" she asked.

"We fly to Camp Atterbury tomorrow morning, so now's our best chance. Join us, please, won't you? How about it?"

Thankful for knowing these two extraordinary people, Colleen nodded and choked out a "yes", then embraced both in a group hug.

The Air Devils Inn seemed familiar territory now, no longer the intimidating place from the past. With shoes sticking on gummy tiles, Colleen led them across the floor to a booth, a journey made nearly impossible by steps up to a narrow doorway and down an aisle not wide enough to accommodate a wheelchair. With help from two officers who lifted the chair over the threshold, then cleared a wide path, Liz wedged herself between tables, where she could be out of everyone's way.

The waiter delivered their drinks, and after he swallowed the first gulp of the cold brew, Van started talking in that insouciant way that Liz had so accurately described. Nothing was off limits as they lazily rolled from one topic to another. Colleen could see why Liz was crazy about her husband, this open minded, principled, curious man.

His love of Liz manifested through his thoughtfulness. He gently touched her, laughed at her comments with unaffected amusement, kept her plate full and offered to refill her glass. In every way, this gallant gentleman doted on this woman he clearly adored, forming an aura around her as she absorbed every kindness, every tender gesture.

Colleen recognized the tinge of envy welling up. *This display of affection, so natural and sincere, is any woman's desire. Why wouldn't I want a taste of that? Will I ever? It never happened with Tommy O'Brien. Will I get another chance?*

By the end of his second beer, Van's conversation became more serious as he answered their questions and described the circumstances surrounding his injuries and capture. His story mesmerized them. Neither interrupted. He could not have continued, if they did.

"I'd been flying missions over New Georgia, multiple runs in the previous weeks as the fighting raged in the South Pacific." He spoke slowly. "I'd just finished my fifteenth and returned the plane to the aircraft carrier.

"Pilots stay prepared 24-7 to provide air cover for the ground troops and sailors, but I was standing on the flight deck with a bunch of guys, thinking I was done for the day. Suddenly, the loudest boom you ever heard exploded all around us. The ship was on fire, cut in two, black smoke so thick you couldn't see or breathe. A Japanese pilot crashed right into us. Parts of his plane and motor got entangled in the ship. The bombs on board made it even worse. One fell between the flight and hangar decks and exploded.

"Our corpsmen tried to reach the wounded, but those isolated by fire on the forecastle, well, their situation was dire. I found a fire extinguisher and made my way forward, dodging flames as I went. Another sailor, manning a seawater firehose with fairly good pressure, scattered the gas fires away from us. By using water and foam alternately, we advanced."

Van took the last swallow of his beer and a deep breath. His head fell forward. Colleen and Liz waited while he gathered his thoughts, reliving the horror of that night. Amid all that sound, only silence. No one spoke.

"We crawled our way up several stairs," he

said softly, voice choked with emotion, "through dark and smoky passageways, along the burning forecastle. The explosion blew many of the crew off the catwalks, off the carrier, into a sea of fire with no life jackets to keep them afloat. Many drowned, ducking under water to avoid flames.

"Another wall of fire trapped more men below and aft of the forecastle area. Aviation gasoline poured down on them from the burning plane on the flight deck above. As many as could leapt into the sea to escape those flames, but some were trapped, unable to jump. They burned alive. We could hear their screams. In my nightmares, I still hear them."

He took another long pause. Colleen wasn't sure he should go on. Then he took Liz's hand, stroked her arm. It gave him the strength he needed.

"The bulkheads grew blistering hot. That's where I got burned." He resumed as if compelled to get it all out, once and for all. "I've never been so scared. The ammunition and small arms locked away below popped from the heat, like strings of firecrackers. With each salvo, more panicky crewmen jumped."

An image formed in Colleen's mind of all he'd withstood, of the terror he'd experienced; shocked by the crash, the fearsome fire and smell of burning flesh, the screams, his buddies dying all around him, his wounds. Where did he find the courage to prevail?

"Our most urgent task," he continued, "the one thing we could do was reach out to the sailors in the water. The waves rolled rough, we had little to offer them to hold onto. Many were so badly injured, they were dead before they hit the sea. A lot who survived the jump prayed to die quickly.

"We dropped the raft into the water and pulled all we could on to it, everyone out of the burning timbers. There weren't many of us left. We floated all night, until a small boat of Japanese fishermen came along and plucked us out of the ocean, the handful that still lived. I don't know how I got to be one of them." Another pause.

"I'm sure glad you did, my darling," said Liz, resting her head on his shoulder.

"Man, who lives like that?" Van continued. "I mean, who flies into a ship? Don't we all have the same will to live? I've thought about this for a while. I can't identify with any man who hates so much he's willing to get himself killed to destroy his enemy. I want to live a whole lot more than I want to hate."

"You will," Liz said. "We're going to Camp Atterbury tomorrow to get our bodies healthy and determine how to live happily ever after. Isn't that what you promised?" she asked.

"You bet it is, Lizzie. I will personally see to it that you live happily ever after."

"Sounds like a miracle that you survived," Colleen said. "You must have a purpose to fulfill." She meant it.

"I really don't know. While the Japs caged me as a prisoner-of-war with nothing to do but exist, no big ideas appealed to me. I dreamed of going home with Lizzie, maybe having kids someday, doing something to make sense out of this topsy turvy world. The Japs gave me no control over what I ate, when I slept, what I did or how they treated me, but I refused to be their prisoner in mind or spirit. I refuse to ever be anyone's prisoner again."

"That has always been true, Van. A free spirt, that is who you are, who you have been."

"The Japs showed me I held absolutely no power, and those who did, reveled in casting very long shadows over those of us who didn't. They frequently, viciously tortured us to make that point, just because they could. Being powerless is an unusual, and very uncomfortable, state for a pilot to accept. Of course, I wanted a means to escape. But when I realized I could control my mind, that no matter what they threw at me, they could never own my thoughts, well, that knowledge gave me the conviction I could take care of myself, no matter what. It was a victory of sorts. It kept me alive."

"How did you get out of there?" Liz asked, barely able to imagine what she's hearing.

"A couple of the Japanese guards fought like scorpions in a bottle. I don't know what they said, but, clearly, they disliked each other intensely. That was a vulnerability we could exploit. I played one against the other to get the essentials we thirsted for and the lay of the land. We couldn't see anything beyond our cages and would still be imprisoned if those Aussies hadn't come along. That was the real miracle. In the middle of the night, they overtook the guards, opened the gates and we ran to the sea. By then, the Japs were up and shooting us from behind. We evaded gunshot in the water and somehow got on a small boat and took off. It's the closest I've ever come to getting shot in the back."

He paused another long moment before speaking. His voice sounded husky and hoarse. "During those months, from when the plane crashed into us until the mates from Australia appeared like saviors, I didn't know if I'd survive, or how. I had little influence over my fate. I knew I was in bad shape and faced my mortality. Fear lost sway over me. Every minute became valuable, even in the dregs of my cell. Ironically, it is our enemy who taught me to live every minute to the fullest, to value life, even there. In an odd sort of way, I'm grateful to them for that." Van looked toward Liz and gave her a wan smile. His effervescence dissipated. He looked exhausted. She rested her head once more on his shoulder. His story hurt her, too.

Colleen recognized their need for rest and suggested she get Liz back to her room. Neither Van nor Liz objected.

After she'd settled Liz in bed, Van sitting by her side, Colleen said the appropriate good-byes followed by multiple rounds of hugs and kisses.

She gathered her things to depart, bearing a look at her friend, her bellwether. She didn't want to spoil the moment by crying in front of them and tried hard to wear a happy face.

Her hand on the doorknob, Colleen turned for one final glance. "Our paths may not cross again soon, Liz, but I shall remember you always as the best example of what a proper nurse can be. I will remember you as my true north."

DISMISSAL

Chapter Twenty-Two

Everyone has the right to life,
liberty and security of person.

UNITED NATIONS UNIVERSAL
DECLARATION OF HUMAN RIGHTS

❋ ❋ ❋

The mail was slow, and Colleen hadn't heard from Mama in a month. Her most urgent wish was for an update on Chloe. She also wanted a report on where Ithaca's men were stationed, so she could pin the location of every one of them on a map that hung on the wall behind her cot. Checking with the new mailroom manager, a civilian woman who had replaced Corporal Martin, she said, "I'm looking for a letter from my Mama, Ginger. I've just got to have a new photograph of my baby girl, Chloe."

"Does your Mama take real pretty pictures?" Ginger asked, distracted by the packages she sorted.

"She sure does, you should see them. Mama's photos capture the genuine Chloe, the essence of her personality. I never understood why my siblings show so little interest in her pictures. Some of them are haunting, all of them are interesting."

The postmistress handed her an envelope, but it bore a Texas return address. She opened and read it immediately. Jeff had penned a happy note, Jenny signed her name beside his with a small daisy drawn at the end of the "y". He wrote Colleen that he'd found a suitable home and settled into a daily routine. They still had lots of kinks to work out, he said, but his recovery progressed, and friends and family abound. They optimistically chose Jen's birthday, February 12, 1944, as the date for their small, private wedding. It made her smile to hear about their good fortune, their state of grace.

In contrast, everyone on base remained somber after the report of the tragic deaths of twenty-nine people in an air crash. Twenty-five of them had trained at Bowman. Thirteen army nurses, twelve enlisted men and a crew of four officers went missing in early November, when they vanished in fog on a flight from Algiers to Italy. Their plane failed to reach its destination. They radioed their last words as the aircraft fell into the Mediterranean Sea. This tragedy devastated her in particular; she had taught those nurses. A month later, her gut still roiled whenever she thought of it.

Since Liz left, she didn't have a confidante to talk things over with. She felt isolated, a little lonely and found herself in the strange position of sharing her own cache of wisdom with the newest recruits. She passed on to them which shower stall door won't close, the better soap to use, how to navigate morning drill sergeants you don't want to mess with and where to get the furnishings to design a bunk like hers. It had evolved into a comfortable oasis doing triple duty as a cozy bedroom, dressing area and parlor all in eight-by-eight square feet.

It seemed odd to be the expert now. It surprised her how quickly she had become comfortable living on an airfield, with huge, flying ambulances roaring in and out, in this superb landscape so far from Ithaca.

She remained dedicated to the mission, thrived on the teamwork and relished the opportunity to teach a fresh group of nurses. Her skills had increased during the overtime shifts at Nichols that satisfied her nursing soul, learning by observing all those so worthy of her sincere regard. She'd grown bold in decision making and using her voice to speak up. Some of the smartest, most committed and caring people she'd ever known offered constant stimulation and supported her professionally as a strong woman and better nurse.

But all of this added together could never take the place of her devotion to Chloe. While her service provided exactly what she needed now, she bore the weight of an endless longing for her daughter. She gave thanks for this opportunity and recognized the salve that saved her in this most unusual setting. Having that to celebrate nudged her into the holiday spirit, despite her grief for the nurses who had lost their lives, despite missing Chloe.

Helen Peak spent Christmas Day on the assembly line making items her husband might use, PFC Phillip Peak, an honorable member of the U.S. Marines. Patricia Stewart spent her holiday inspecting tent fabrics at the Jeffersonville, Indiana Quartermaster Depot. Lucy Lincoln organized medical supplies at a Louisville warehouse.

The Colonel announced that Bowman Field would have no interruption to the daily schedule on Christmas, except that some of his staff would join the enlisted men for a meatless dinner served on mess hall trays.

The Colonial Dames of the Commonwealth of Kentucky thought otherwise. They planned an elaborate program from four to seven to entertain residents at Bowman. Determined that every soldier in Nichols hospital know that people cared, they scheduled student violinists to stroll the halls playing carols like *I'll Be Home for Christmas* and Bing Crosby's hit, *Winter Wonderland*. Volunteers hung garlands in every room.

The public had donated items into barrels sitting around the city, and the elderly ladies of the bingo clubs wrapped them as gifts using glittery gold paper with satin ribbons and perky green bows, one for each of the twenty-six nurses and one hundred and seventy patients. High school kids decorated eight trees, one for every ward, each designed around a unique theme. The students cut five hundred brilliantly colored flowers and hung them on the walls, using bandages for tape, along with glittering red, white and blue stars to brighten the halls without the use of electric lights.

Other volunteers addressed thousands of cards to local servicemen and those overseas. The Red Cross distributed cartons of lifesavers to the men, who received them with the childish delight of a kid in a candy shop, eager to trade with their buddies for their favorite colors. The Gray Ladies set up a booth in the hospital lobby for the convenience of the patients to shop for their loved ones, then prepared their purchased gifts for mailing.

"Doggonit! I broke the zipper in my skirt," Colleen sighed as she dressed for the celebration.

"Well, it's ruined, unless you can melt and mold metal," said Rita, who held out another one for Colleen to try.

"I'd rather mold a good cup of coffee," she said, taking the skirt and trying it on, a perfect fit.

"Me, too. I'd give up my big toe if there was also a dollop of cream in it."

"Two weeks ago, when the mess ran out, just might be the longest day of the war."

"Yeah, that long day could last until the bitter end, according to the cook."

"Do you suppose the Germans are out of coffee, too? Maybe they'd be willing to call a truce until we find some."

"How can you possibly fight a war without it?"

"Perhaps that's how we end this. Deprive everyone of their cup of joe and don't give them any more, until everyone agrees to quit and go home."

The nurses finished dressing, then wrapped themselves in coats and their patients in blankets and rolled them to the convent chapel for Mass. Afterwards, the good nuns would offer a lovely reception just for the nurses, serving herb teas brewed steamy hot and pastries baked especially for the occasion. Mass seemed too long as they anticipated the sweet-smelling treats sitting on fine china in the dining room. Place cards with hand-painted names sat waiting for them on the festive silver and gold tablecloths. They were eager to oblige.

As Colleen returned the men back to their beds to rest before the program, the boys all said, "Good day, Nurse" in unison, thinking it a funny joke on her. But when she replied, "Good day, lads, rest well," it meant something entirely different to her.

Standing there, smiling at them all, she realized in caring for these men, she had discovered a lost part of herself. Stoic Colleen, who had borne the insults, excused the drinking and slunk to the floor under the force of a fist still spoke occasionally as a small whisper in her head, but it was considerably softer and easier to dismiss. Cracking through that shattered façade, she had reclaimed the intrepid girl she used to be, the one who fearlessly climbed trees and insisted on playing baseball with her brothers, not softball with her sisters. She understood just how much she had submerged her personality, her goals, her speech, to inhabit a marriage based on Tommy's views and governed by his rules. She understood how hard she'd worked to recover from it.

Overseeing this room full of grateful guys, all of whom looked to her leadership to promote their recovery, she knew she could never again be that woman who was willing to take a punch to keep the peace and her husband. She vowed to protect this Colleen and grow her to maturity.

On her way to the reception, she stopped by the library, which the Woman's Club had turned into another holiday mecca. They had trimmed trees given by the Red Cross and woven scarlet ribbons through wreaths three feet wide that hung on the front doors. The convalescing veterans who could, had freely indulged in making crafts to send home as tokens of their love and healing. Miss Vernon organized stockings for the patrons and found small items to fill them. No one was forgotten on Christmas.

Miss Vernon also filled the bookcases in the small room Jeff had used with a fine assortment of books. Earnest Hemingway's *For Whom the Bell Tolls* sat displayed on the top shelf. She'd added rocking chairs to the front porch. On this temperate Christmas Day, the sun shone brightly as men covered in blankets gathered in wheelchairs to soak it in.

Pilots and nurses lined up with pool cues to face the white ball and hit a striped one into a pocket in the lone pool table. The click, click of crashing balls joined the laughter of others sitting at tables of four playing cards, swearing and laughing as the games went on.

Colleen checked the bulletin board to see when President Roosevelt would address the nation tonight. Many would gather at the library after the Christmas program to listen to the radio. The determination in the President's voice inspired determination in the people. His knack for explaining complicated situations, and the plans to address them, gave courage to everyone. He offered jaunty words of advice in a manner that consoled the public. Colleen was eager to hear him talk. It would be late when she returned to the barracks.

The next day, Captain Dorsey commanded her to report to his office at 0900.

"Nurse O'Brien," he said in his no nonsense

tone of voice, "I have become aware that one Thomas J. O'Brien, Ithaca, New York, formerly the foreman at the Burnett Rope factory, has been drafted into the United States Army. He's to report to Camp Edwards for basic training in two weeks. That is your husband, correct?"

"Yes, sir."

"Your year of service is nearly up. You're a few weeks from your anniversary. Wrap things up here, Nurse O'Brien, so that you can return home before your husband's service begins."

"Thank-you sir, I appreciate your consideration. My daughter lives with my parents. She's well cared for. I miss her terribly, but sir, I intend to finish the commitment I made. I'll serve out the remaining weeks and complete my full term. I'd like to leave with honor, sir."

"Nurse O'Brien, you misunderstand. This is not a suggestion, it's an order. Go home, with honor. Uncle Sam does not want both parents to be in service in the war simultaneously. Your husband has been called to duty. His call precludes yours. You will return home to Ithaca."

"But sir, I need this job."

"You will find employment in Ithaca."

"Yes, sir, I suppose I will."

"Then do so. If you want to be a patriot, Nurse O'Brien, grow a victory garden and save your scrap metal. Better still, teach your daughter how to be a proper citizen."

"I will, sir."

"Your term ends Friday at the conclusion of your class. Nurse Marcy Statler will take your place. Meet with her, bring her up to speed. Thank-you for your service, Nurse O'Brien. Dismissed."

Just like that, with his decree, her commitment to the U.S. armed forces concluded. Could she go back to civilian life? Swing dancing and the jitterbug? Swirling skirts and sweater sets? Turned down socks and saddle shoes? After seeing men and women dressed in the crisp uniforms of the military, everything else seemed silly. She wouldn't miss the powdered milk or tins of Vienna sausages and would gladly trade them for Mama's pot roast and potatoes or spicy Irish stew. But his decision disappointed her. She regretted being forced to leave her post.

HORIZON

Chapter Twenty-Three

All Human Beings Are Free and Equal.

UNITED NATIONS UNIVERSAL
DECLARATION OF HUMAN RIGHTS

❊ ❊ ❊

O n Tuesday, the mother of a missing hero, who was presumed dead, accepted a medal on his behalf at a small ceremony at Bowman Field. Colonel Jenkins presented Mrs. A. J. Olivet the award on behalf of her son, Andrew, after he distinguished himself as a navigator in a heavy bombardment group. The Colonel said the award represented our nation's gratitude towards, and pride in, Lieutenant Olivet. His mother accepted the medal and salute, knowing it meant she would exchange the blue star in her window for a gold one, because her son was dead. A five-plane formation flew overhead, with one peeling off as the others moved onward.

Colleen attended these poignant ceremonies whenever she could and wept at each one, the enormity of their loss an emotional reminder of the cost of war. The symbolism provided a moving tribute. It seemed the least she could do, to honor the men who gave their lives and venerate them with their families. Only a small crowd attended on a busy workday. Colleen noticed that Mrs. Olivet stood alone. At the conclusion, she walked to her and extended a hand.

"Hello, Mrs. Olivet. I'm Nurse Colleen O'Brien, here to honor your son, Andrew. Please know we recognize his sacrifice, and yours. Accept our sincere thanks for his dedication."

Mrs. Olivet transferred the folded flag from her right hand to her left and took Colleen's in a firm grip. "Thank you, Nurse. Andrew loved being in the service, said it made him feel a part of something big and important, pretty special for a small-town boy from Harmony, Arkansas."

"He was special. We have great respect for him. I hope you see that."

"Oh, I do, Nurse, but not because of this. My Andrew was worthy of respect long before he joined up."

"I'm sure he was, Mrs. Olivet. I'd like to hear why. Can I get you a cup of coffee before you catch the bus back to Arkansas? It's not fancy, it's not even coffee. We ran out weeks ago. It'll be whatever beverage the mess has on hand. But it will give us a chance to get acquainted, for you to tell me his story, if you are so inclined."

"I'd like that," she said. Together they headed in the direction of the dining hall.

They settled around a corner table. Colleen served them both a glass of juice then found a bowl of peanuts to munch and share. It was easy to get Mrs. Olivet, Elaine, to speak of Andrew. She spent the next hour describing the forts he built in the backyard and the night he hit the winning homerun that ended at the Dairy Castle with root beer floats for the whole team. Andrew's favorite furry friend, "Banjo," the mutt he rescued, snoozes on his bed still, waiting for Andrew's return.

"Andrew is not my first big loss," she said. "I buried my husband, Anthony, seven months ago. He was with me here today, though."

"Gosh, how awful that you must endure this tragedy alone. It must be hard to get through something like this by yourself," said Colleen.

"It's been tough. Most days I don't know how I do it. I just keep going. Neither of them would want me to give up before my time."

"That takes real courage to keep living after such loss."

"I don't have much choice. Andrew was my only child."

"You have lost everything."

"There is one thing I have, one thing no one can take from me."

"Oh? What is it?"

"The ability to use what little authority I

possess to live honestly and with love."

"How can you keep a positive attitude in the midst of your disappointment?"

"What is the alternative? I can't ask something different from a situation that has nothing different to offer. Hanging on to what used to be won't solve this problem. It won't allow me to prepare for what I must do next."

"How do you let go of the past? Of all your dreams and plans?"

"I figured out after Anthony died that wanting what you can't have blocks you from enjoying what you can have, what you may actually need. I guess I don't assume as much as I once did. I just try to stay one step ahead of what life demands of me. I've had to muster up a resilient spirit to keep going during this madness, to overcome what it's cost me."

"Then I wish we could all muster that same resilient spirit. I could certainly use it. I'm still trying to recover from a split from my husband that occurred almost a year ago."

"Look for it, Nurse, you'll find it in yourself. You are a woman with a big heart. You have the passion to support it."

"It's difficult, when you don't see a clear path forward."

"You bet it is. It's taken me awhile to understand that sorrow has something to teach me. First, I learned how to bear it. Then it became clear that anger, hatred, self-pity, that baggage is too heavy to carry around. Sometimes we hang on to those things even when they hurt us, because it's all we know. After Anthony died, I tried desperately to hang on, but finally had to let go of the despair just to feel human again. Guess now I'll start over."

"How will you do it?"

"I don't know. It won't be easy; it won't be quick. I don't know for sure that I can. I'll need to find a reason to hope every day. That will require patience as I prioritize what's still important. It will require me to release all that weighs me down. If I can figure out how to do that, I might be free again, free enough to find my next calling. That's all I have left to claim, since I am no longer wife or mother. Maybe that will be a life worth living. Maybe I can still become the person I want to be. On my best days, when I use my imagination, that is the vision I hold."

Colleen absorbed her words and took hold of her arm. *She is so brave.* Here was a woman who somehow used her brokenness to learn, then shared her wisdom through her touch, her smile and her words. Her brokenness did not define her; honesty, integrity and compassion did.

When Elaine indicated it was time to leave for the bus that would take her home, Colleen perceived a special kinship with this eloquent woman. As their conversation concluded, standing with her purse over her arm and coat draped over her shoulders, Elaine turned to

Colleen and spoke, almost as an afterthought.

"One thing I learned teaching science to eighth graders, Colleen, is that the natural world is a cornucopia of incredible complexity and variety. There are 248 separate muscles in the head of an ordinary caterpillar, for example. The Brazilian rain forest has 2.5 million different species of insects flying under its canopy. Humans possess about 25,000 genes, the same number, more or less, as a mustard plant. And our Creator must have really liked beetles. We have thousands of varieties. I mean, really, who needs more than one or two?"

"Good point, but they must be here for a reason."

"Exactly, they have a purpose. Now, these organisms produce more seeds and offspring than they need. Each one is genetically different. Those that survive are stronger and pass on their best traits to the next generation."

"Yes, I get the theory of evolution, but what does that have to do with Andrew?"

"Well, my point is that genetic diversity is fundamental to life. It's nature's insurance policy that assures our continued existence through the advantage of natural selection. Environments change, diseases come and go, but we have lasted because diversity equips us to adapt. It has existed in every form from the first moment of the universe. Each of us is part of that diversity. Surely, if this is the divine plan for our world, our quest is to simply accept what is. When we do, our differences become cause for celebration, not an excuse to fight. When we learn to value those differences, boys like my Andrew won't have to die."

On her last full day at Bowman, following class, Colleen borrowed a bike and rode past Jack, the camp gardener, as he tidied the quadrangle without disturbing the hundreds of tulip bulbs he so diligently planted last autumn. Flags flew in the breeze. A light dusting of snow turned the world white.

This memory will stay with me forever, seeing planes on the runway flying out of here, one after the other, she thought, feeling empowered by her own strength. *Some carry nurses I trained to their first assignments. Some carry pilots practicing for a war they're determined to win. Some carry men and women who will never return.*

She followed the streets along the river. As the evening grew dark, a half-moon slipped over the horizon. Faint lights blinked across a dainty, gingerbread neighborhood. In a nearby park, players joined a basketball game already in the second quarter, interrupted by the sound of wild geese honking overhead.

Mist rose from a field and drifted into a tiny stretch of woods beyond, the air cold, the smell of damp earth mingled with whiffs of smoke. Beyond a ridge of skyline lay the rim of the world, the place where ideas are born. Colleen heard the Atlantic roaring in her memory and recalled the giant searchlights in the harbor flashing across the sky. *Do they search for me*?

As they parted ways, Mrs. Olivet had said, "There is nothing that is too much to bear, Colleen, if you can figure out something good that remains. But you do have to be willing to give up being a caterpillar, if you want to become a butterfly."

Colleen discovered that it's a huge relief to stop denying everything that had happened and start accepting reality. She felt the tension melt away when she began to be honest with herself. She could see the destructive patterns holding her back; acquiescing somehow to physical assault, so frantic to keep the peace was she. Her willingness to silence herself, to give up her own thoughts to avoid conflict. Her denial of her own truths to enable Tommy to force his version on her.

Mrs. Olivet had said that we each contain the correct combination of genes from our parents to become a unique person, one who has never been seen before, who will never be seen again. "Just think of it! Each person is distinct, original, created only for here and now. We must have a purpose, too, just like every one of those beetles."

That will be my new mission, Colleen said softly to herself, clamoring to live free, *to find my purpose in this crazy world and commit to it. Whatever it may be, I know for sure it begins with my Chloe.*

She trembled with single-minded attention

as she pictured her daughter's face, heard her giggles, felt the softness of her skin and smelled its sweetness. Her posture straightened, inspired by Mrs. Olivet's example. How could she forgive Tommy? How could she let go of all that enraged her? The loss of her marriage. The life she thought was hers.

I don't have the answers now, but I do know the first step. I will go to Chloe. I will hold her in my arms. We will grow our lives together. I will seek my destiny. I will live what I believe.

*****

Colleen rocked lazily with Chloe in the porch swing two days before her twenty-third birthday. The mailman handed her an envelope, a card from Liz. She reached in for a folded piece of sturdy, white cardboard, the slick kind you pull from the bottom of a shoebox. On the cover, Liz had drawn in black ink a lovely silhouette of a mother and daughter, heads tilted in song, sitting together on a front porch much like the one they sat on now. The beauty of it inspired tears.

Inside, Liz's dainty print described the details of her life with Van. Colleen devoured every one. The best info she saved for last. "I'm writing with my right hand, have improved enough to return to work. You'll never guess where. The Army Air Corps wants me back! We proved flight nurses should remain a permanent part of the military, and the brass agrees. They're starting another training school in Texas, bigger than Bowman, and asked me to set it up and run it. What an honor! The nurse who couldn't get in, opening doors for others. Van will join me in about three weeks, the minute he is commissioned. Will let you know then, but he likes his chances."

Colleen read further, all the good news, and smiled. She sipped her tea, savored the moment and pictured her friend. She read each word again slowly and placed them next to her heart, then opened her arms. Chloe encircled her in a sacred gesture of healing love.

*****

ABOUT THE AUTHOR

Dana Walker Lindley

 Ms. Lindley worked as an aide to a U. S. Senator and in management for Meredith Corporation, publisher of Better Homes and Gardens books. Her byline has appeared in more than twenty publications including the Newport Daily News, Family Times, Newsweek.com, Unity Magazine, the Intercultural Writer's Review, the News-Gazette of Champaign-Urbana and the Cincinnati Enquirer.

Her first novel, Cameo, centers on Mary McMahon Donnelley's story, set in the 1900 Galveston hurricane. Ascension is the second in the series about her daughter, Colleen Donnelley O'Brien, a nurse in service during World War II. Kinship tells the story of granddaughter Dr. Chloe O'Brien McGuire, set in Kenya in 1985.

ACKNOWLEDGEMENTS

Inspiration:
The doctors and nurses who treated the wounded during World War II

Information:
Bowman Field
Louisville Courier - Journal Archives
Filson Historical Society
Louisville Free Public Library
Crescent Hill Woman's Club

Insight:
Madge Brown
Melanie Bloemer
Cate Heady
Eric Schmall

Imagination:
Katherine Lindley

Made in the USA
Monee, IL
26 February 2023

28487476R00156